IN LOVE WE TRUST

SKY EM

IN LOVE WE TRUST:

LUCK & STORM 2

Sky EM

Copyright © 2020 Sky EM
Published by Crowned BAWSE Publications
Cover Design: Sky EM
Interior Design: Sky EM
ISBN-13: 978-1-7328886-1-6

Crowned BAWSE

SkyEM@CrownedBAWSE.com

Ordering Information:
Quantity sales. Special discounts are available on quantity purchases by corporations, associations, and others. For details, contact the publisher at the e-mail address above.

Printed in the United States of America

This book is dedicated to you, Daddy! I know if you were here, you'd want a printed copy (that you wouldn't read) just to put up with all the rest. My first printed copy is yours, Old Man.
Thank you for the last fourteen months. I'd give anything to rush to you from work just to sit bedside with you while we said nothing... just watching the news. I love and miss you so, so much...

Love, your baby!

"TEARS FALLING LIKE THE WATERS WHEN THE LEVEES DROPPED."

-Meek Mill

"Babe!" Storm could hear Luck screaming for her throughout the house, but she couldn't answer him. She was grief stricken and confused as she sat with slumped shoulders at the foot of their neatly made bed, thinking about the words that the doctor had told her earlier. Tears streamed down her face, heavy with sadness as her breathing became stagnant, getting caught in her chest. *There is no way that this is happening to me again. What am I doing wrong? What's wrong with me?* she thought to herself.

"Storm, you ain't hear me callin' your ass?" Luck fussed as he walked into the bedroom that the two of them shared. He was home early, in a playful mood and looking forward to spending time with her before Lauryn got home later. As of late, his schedule had been keeping him away from Storm and Lauryn more than he liked.

The second he looked at Stormie's face, all of that changed, though. Lucky's face turned cold as he rushed to be close to her, damn near tripping over his feet. Kneeling, he got down on one knee, directly in front of her, putting her face between his hands and forcing Storm to look at him instead of at her hands as she'd been previously doing.

"What's wrong?" Kissing Storm on her forehead first before he moved to her nose and then her lips. Afterwards, Luck tried to be patient as he stared at her, waiting for a response. Although his affection was meant to make her feel comfortable enough to tell him what was wrong, it caused her to cry harder. "Stormie, baby... you got to tell me what's wrong."

"I'm... I'm pregnant." She was finally able to blurt out through the dry heaves. They had been trying for the past three and a half years to get pregnant and had been unsuccessful. The few times that Storm did end up pregnant, it ended badly, just like this pregnancy was also ending badly.

"Why are you crying? This is what we've wanted for years." Confusion was evident on his face for a second before it dawned on him what was coming next. *Shit, not again,* he thought to himself.

Shaking her head, no, Stormie prepared herself to tell him what he had already figured out was wrong. "It's another ectopic pregnancy. We caught it in time though... The doctor gave me a Methotrexate shot to stop the pregnancy. I have to go back in four days to do blood work so she can make sure that it's working. If it doesn't, I have to get the surgery to remove the other tube."

It looked like the wind had been knocked out of Luck as he sat there staring at her briefly before hugging her and whispering affirmations that everything would be okay.

"I can't go through this again..." This would be the second ectopic pregnancy that Storm had gone through, not to mention the five miscarriages that she'd already had. "I give up... I'm— I'm just going to... If the medicine works, I'm just gonna go and get my tube tied." She hesitated and stuttered to get it out, but she got it out, eventually.

"No, the hell you're not, Storm." Luck exclaimed, jumping to his feet before the words were even fully out of her mouth.

Immediately, rage consumed Storm replacing the hurt and sadness that had been present just seconds before. "It's my body, Luciano. I can't keep going through these disappointments and putting my body through this strain. Every single time I wind up pregnant, I'm so fucking happy and then the minute I miscarry or have to terminate, I'm miserable again. I can't do this anymore. It's taking a toll on me."

"Your body is my body too, Stormie, and you aren't the only one going through the disappointments and depressions after-ward. We both want another baby; you aren't the only one. You're being selfish as fuck right now." Luck moved across the room from where he had been standing in front of her. She could see the hurt and frustration on his face, but Storm needed him to feel her hurt and frustration as well.

"No, you aren't the one going through these fucking surgery's and injections. You aren't the one in physical pain before and after them, you don't have to worry about the side effects from this fucking medicine. I got to stay in the house for the next three days because of this fucking medicine. Not to mention the cramps, diarrhea, mouth sores, and hair loss I have experienced and can possibly experience now because of this shot. Don't tell me about you going through this shit with me because you're not.

3

You are here, yes... you are beside me while I go through it, but you aren't going through it with me." Storm stood up and began pacing along the foot of their bed. "I got to miss work, miss out on time with our baby girl, hell, miss time with you too."

Luck was staring at Storm with turbulence evident in his face. "That's the most selfish shit you've ever said to me." He was frozen with disbelief temporarily. "Had someone asked me before today if my wife was selfish, I would have told them nah. Shit, I would have told them hell nah, but I can't honestly say that shit now." He chuckled and then looked at Storm for a minute like he was trying to get his thoughts together before he said the wrong thing. "I may not be in physical pain, but I'm in mental and emotional pain right along with you. I got to watch my wife suffer and know that it's nothing I can do. I'm the one running around making sure you're comfortable and that you have every-thing you need. I'm the one staying up all-night listening to you moan and groan in your sleep. Making sure Lauryn doesn't know anything is wrong with mommy, making sure that she still gets everything she needs. I make sure that the only thing you have to do is rest and use the bathroom, clearing my schedule for weeks to make sure you're good." Shaking his head in anger and frustra-tion, he headed to the bedroom door before stopping to say. "Do whatever the fuck you want to do, though... you're right, it's your body and I'm not in no *physical* pain with you."

Lucky left Storm standing there, staring at his back as he walked out on her. Seconds later, the front door could be heard slamming before she broke down in tears again. Walking to the side of the bed that Stormie occupied daily, she plopped down on the bed before reaching for her cell phone that was sitting on her nightstand.

With tears clouding her vision and a sinking feeling in her chest, Stormie called Amber, needing to vent. Waiting for Amber to answer, she cleaned her face with the back of her arm and laid back on the bed. After two rings, Amber sent Stormie to voicemail. Blowing out a frustrated breath, Stormie muttered, "Answer, Am..." Voice cracking along the way. Hanging up, she called her right back. When she was sent to voicemail again, she hung up and called Amber back a third time before finally getting an answer.

"Storm, I'm doing a client's head..." Amber said, not bothering to say hello.

"I need you," Storm croaked out to her.

Hearing the distress in Storm's voice, she immediately stopped what she was doing to aid her best friend and sister. *"Shit, hold on."* Talking could be heard in the background before a door slammed and everything got silent. *"What's going on, Stormie? What's wrong?"*

"Another ectopic pregnancy... Luck and I just got into a horrible argument. I can't keep going through this disappointment. Maybe we're supposed to just have Lauryn."

"I'm so sorry, Storm." Even though Amber was good with her one for the moment, she knew how much Storm and Luck wanted another baby. She couldn't imagine the stress and sadness that came from trying for so long and not being granted the one thing you wanted. They could buy just about everything they wanted, but this wasn't one of those things. *"They can't tell you what's wrong? This is your second ectopic pregnancy."*

"They gave me some bullshit possible causes but none of them apply to me."

"There has to be a specialist that you can go to who can give you more information."

"I don't know and at this point, Am, I don't even care. I give up. We've been trying to get pregnant for years now and it's always something."

"Maybe you guys should just let things happen on God's timing."

"Lauryn is about to be six next month, Amber. How much longer are we supposed to wait?"

"Until God says it's time..."

"Well, I have no more patience. I told Lucky I was getting my tube tied."

"You did what?!"

"You heard me... I'm over this shit."

"Stormie, you can't just tell him something like that. That's your husband... that's something the two of you should have talked about and agreed on together. Besides that, we all know how much Lucky wants more children, hell, we know how bad you yourself want more children. Don't do something permanent based off of how you're feeling right now at this moment. You don't want to hate yourself or have Lucky resenting you in the future either."

"I'm gonna hate myself if I keep trying with these same results, Amber. I already know what the outcome is gonna be, why keep punishing myself like this?"

"You don't know anything besides how the previous times have ended. I get it, it's frustrating and depressing, but just imagine if a year or two from now you find yourself really wanting a baby. What are you gonna do then?"

"There is always adoption... there are so many children out here without parents."

"It's not the same and you know it, Storm. How many times have you said that to me when I suggested that the two of you adopt?" Rolling her eyes as if Amber could see her, Storm blew out a breath of frustration before sitting back on the bed. *"Where is Luck? Maybe he can talk some sense into you."*

"Your guess is as good as mine. He left after I told him my decision and he threw a tantrum."

"Not a tantrum, Storm. It's his feelings. He has a right to feel like that. That's not a decision you make on your own."

"Why not? I'm the one who has to experience all of this shit, not him."

"Bullshit, you think he's not going through the same fucking motions as you? I'm sorry but you sound stupid, Stormie."

"You know what... bye, Amber." Not giving her a chance to respond, Storm hung up on her and threw her phone towards the foot of the bed.

Why the fuck was no one else understanding what she was going through, was all that she could think about. Storm was sure that Lucky was hurting but he wasn't hurting anything like she was. Stormie had lost sleep countless nights behind these miscarriages and ectopic pregnancies. She was the one study questioning what was wrong with her, not Lucky. He just didn't understand. Every time she found out that she was pregnant, it was like a light lit up her entire world. Then the light would be shut out without warning each time.

The first time that Storm had gotten pregnant, she made it all the way to her sixth month before she miscarried. Luck and Storm had designed the nursery for their son, bought all of these little clothes, and toys just to have to box it all up and put it in the garage. The pain was excruciating to have to deliver a stillborn, and then the mental pain afterwards was incomparable. Nothing could have prepared her for any of that...

Storm laid around for a few more hours battling her thoughts and asking God the same questions she had been asking him for years before getting up and going to get Lauryn from school. If nothing else did, she had to admit that on the days when life became a bit too much for her, Lauryn gave her joy and hope.

. . .

"HEY BEAUTIFUL," Storm smiled at her the second that Lauryn was in her view.

"Mommy, I missed you." Lauryn said after running to her mother and hugging her. Storm held onto her hand as they made their way out of the school to her truck.

"I missed you more. How was school today?"

"Good."

"What did you learn?"

"How to color in the lines." Lauryn said, causing her mother to laugh.

"That's all you learned, little girl?" Shaking her head, Storm laughed some more as she buckled Lauryn into her booster seat.

"I know you had to learn more than just that... no math? No words?" With a grin on her face, Lauryn shook her head no once again. "Nuh-huh little girl... there's no way we're paying all this money for you to go to this school and they're only teaching you how to color in the lines. But I'll let you make it today." Closing the door after securing Lauryn in her seat, she walked around to the driver's side and climbed in the car. "What do you want to eat tonight?" Not feeling like cooking, Storm was begging the universe that Lauryn would choose something that she could pick up instead of something that she would have to cook.

"Can we have pizza tonight?"

"We sure can," Storm was quick to respond. Pizza was right up her alley. Driving to the local pizza shop, she parked and sat in the car to order the food by phone. Ordering two pizza pies and some buffalo wings, she got comfortable afterwards while listening to Lauryn talk for a while about a little bit of everything. Storm was amazed at how smart Lauryn was at only five. She was so inquisitive and understood way more than Storm could remember understanding at her age.

Stealing glances at Lauryn through the rearview mirror,

Storm admired her baby girl. She was the perfect blend of her and Luck. With a rich soft brown complexion, wide almond shaped eyes that resembled hers were mixed with hazel and green like her father. Her chubby cheeks had deep dimples that complemented her pretty smile that Storm swore she'd gotten from Luck but Luck claimed she'd gotten from her. Her thick bushy eyebrows had long ago connected faintly, making it one eyebrow but most people didn't notice it. Her natural coils were pulled up in two bushy ponytails wrapped up in moon buns per Lauryn's request this morning. She was slim and long just as Storm had been growing up as well.

Storm loved seeing who her and Luck had created— seeing what features she got from who, what personality traits she inherited from them each. She wanted nothing more than to have more children and see who they became, who they looked more like... who they acted more like.

"Come on, pretty girl. Let's go and get this pizza." Getting out of the car, Storm went to open Lauryn's car door and held it open as she waited for Lauryn to unbuckle her seatbelt before she climbed out of the car.

For some reason, it was packed inside of the pizza shop with two people still waiting for their pick-up orders. Lauryn was keeping Storm occupied though, busy telling her all about her birthday plans with her friends while the two stood against the wall waiting for the line to move.

When Lauryn had talked until she couldn't talk anymore, Storm decided to waste some time by heading over to her Instagram. In the midst of Lauryn finding something else to talk about, Storm snapped a video of her and captioned it 'My heart is turning six soon' before sharing it to her Insta-story.

Within seconds, Luck had viewed the story. In the seconds that followed, he shared a picture of him, Storm, and Lauryn and captioned it *"My 25 to Life, my family, my strength and weakness... doesn't matter what we go through, we're going to always pull through as long as we have each other. I love you both!"* Instantly, a smile was put on Storm's face and the despair that she had been feeling thanks to their argument, was replaced. Instead of commenting on it, she liked it before reposting it to her feed with his caption, adding one of her own above his. *"There was no other option... We love you more!"*

WALKING in the house with Lauryn in tow and the food that they had just picked up, Storm was disappointed to see that Lucky wasn't back yet. Instead of dwelling on it, she headed straight to the kitchen so that she could put the pizzas down and prepare for dinner.

"Lau, go put your book bag down and then wash your hands. I'll meet you in the living room when you're finished." She told Lauryn as she washed her hands in the kitchen sink before she grabbed two plates, a knife, and two cups. Walking into the living room with them, Storm was stopped by the front door opening.

Even though her and Lucky had sort of made amends, there were still so much more that needed to be said. Butterflies fluttering in her stomach caused Storm to temporarily loose her thoughts. She watched, still frozen in place, as Luck walked in the house, placing his keys on the table in the foyer.

"Hey," Instead of moving all the way into the room, he stopped short, observing her with questioning eyes. Looking into his eyes, she could see that he was still thinking about the argument the two of them had gotten into earlier, just as she was. Even though Storm stood firm in her decision to get her tubes tied, she didn't want to talk about that right now. Right now, she wanted to have dinner with her family and focus on the now. Later, they could talk about what she knew would not be an easy conversation.

"Hey, I got pizza for dinner..." She told him, not sure what else to say.

"Cool... where's Lau?"

"Washing her hands." Shaking his head, he slowly made his way towards Storm before wrapping her up in his arms. The resolve that had previously lived in Storm melted away with just his touch.

"I don't wanna argue anymore," Luck said before placing a kiss on her cheek.

"Me either, but this is something we have to talk about." It would have been easier to carry on like nothing was going on, but she knew that nothing would get resolved if they just swept this under the rug. "It doesn't have to be today Lucky, but it has to happen."

Shaking his head, he acknowledged that he had heard her before walking away to get himself ready for dinner as well. That wasn't a conversation he felt they needed to have, he would never agree with her doing that to her body, but he would say anything to have some peace at the moment.

"Hello?" Sleep was evident in Storm's voice. Accompanying a headache that was taking over her being, Storm also had a throat full of sandpaper. Her and Luck had been up most of the night; her throwing up and him holding her hair and cleaning up behind her. They were both exhausted.

"Hey Sis, I'm sorry for waking you. I just wanted to check on you. How are you?" Even though Amber said she was calling to check on Storm, Storm could hear something in Am's tone. She didn't

know what it was but whatever it was, Stormie was gonna find out.

"I'm tired, truthfully. I was up all night throwing up. I probably went to sleep an hour or two ago. What's wrong?" Throwing the covers off of her, Storm slowly sat up and threw her legs over the side of the bed.

"How do you—never mind. Your brother is what's wrong."

"I figured, what did he do this time?"

"He went out last night and came in around two in the morning. That wasn't a problem. I don't expect him to come in at nine or ten at night. He doesn't have a curfew... the problem is that he decides to stop in the bathroom downstairs on his way up. I didn't think anything of it at first, I'm thinking maybe his ass had too much to drink and had to pee really bad or something." Shaking her head as if Amber could see her, Storm made her way to the bathroom with her attention fixated on the phone. *"Well the water was running in the sink for about five minutes, he was moving from the basement to the bathroom and back. So, I get up to go see what's going on... I'm thinking this nigga sick or some shit but instead, I walk in on this motherfucker washing his dick."*

"You're lying!"

"Bitch, I wish I was. The nigga was washing his fucking dick!"

"Well, what did you do?" Knowing how crazy Amber was, there was no doubt in Storm's mind that her brother was somewhere recovering from the beatdown that she had put on him.

"What could I do? I was so stuck all I could do was ask him what he was doing."

"That's it?!" Storm couldn't believe it.

"Yeah... I'm tired of fighting, Sis. I opened the bathroom door and scared the shit out of him. He couldn't even hold himself up he was so drunk. I asked him what he was doing and he told me he was washing up because he was sweaty. I didn't even bother arguing with him. I just

shook my head and went back to bed. About ten minutes later, he came upstairs, got undressed, and climbed in bed behind me."

Unsure of what to say, Storm forced out a muttered "damn". Mentally, she was preparing herself for the phone call she would be placing to Steven the second she was off the phone with Amber.

"Damn is right. All these years later, a whole wedding, and a baby and this nigga is still up to the same shit he was up to when we were teenagers." Amber fussed.

Storm could understand her frustrations. Steven had taken Amber through hell and back when they were younger. Phone calls from different females, being approached by females about Steven, STD's, pictures, walking in on him and other females, and more; Amber had been through it all. Back then though, Amber was up for the fight, she actually used to get a kick out of it. Every time Steven would fuck up Amber would fuck him up and if the girl he was dealing with jumped bad then she would be the next to get it. Many times, Storm was caught up in the mix thanks to Amber being her best friend. If Storm was around, there was no such thing as a fair fight... didn't matter if it was a one on one or not, Storm was jumping in.

"I don't even know what to say, Am."

"You and me either... I just know that when I walk this time, it's forever."

"You're really thinking about leaving?"

"What else am I gonna do, Storm? I've fought, I've stuck it out, I've tried to be understanding, I've cheated back thinking it would make him see what I was feeling... I've done all the shit I could think about doing. Maybe leaving him is what I need to do."

"I can't believe he's back on that shit again. I really thought that time had taught him and helped him grow up." A few days ago, Storm and Steven had spoken and he had told her how happy he was,

with life, Autumn and Amber. Clearly, that had all been a lie. Storm couldn't believe that he would give everything up just for a moment of pleasure with someone who she was sure meant nothing to him.

"Well, believe it. I'm just gonna let this shit play out the way it's supposed to. Everything done in the dark comes to the fore front... all I gotta do is be patient."

"You're right about that... but in the meantime, I'm calling that brother of mines and telling him about himself."

"Don't even bother. I swear, I'm not pressed over it. I'm hurt, but I'll get over this shit."

"You know I'm still gonna say something. He's dead ass wrong." Making her way to the bathroom, Storm got comfortable on the toilet. Releasing her bladder, she thought about what she would do had it been her and Luck going through this situation and a shiver ran through her body. *I'd kill him. "Yeah, as soon as we get off this phone I'm calling Steven and telling him about himself."*

The conversation between the two ladies carried on for another ten minutes before they decided to get off the phone. Storm wanted to get back in bed while Amber had a head to do.

The second the phone call was disconnected; Storm was dialing Steven's number. While waiting for him to answer, she headed downstairs to the kitchen to get herself a glass of water and a rice cake to snack on. Hitting the last stair, she was surprised to see Luck laying across the couch, asleep. Walking over to him with the phone positioned between her ear and her shoulder, she stared at him for a while, admiring his handsomeness. He had recently gotten a haircut and his lineup was on point. His pink pouty lips were slightly ajar, showing just a glimpse of his perfect teeth. His high yellow skin was smooth and blemish free, only displaying the goatee that adorned his face.

Leaning over, she ran her right hand across his face before

saying his name. "Baby," shaking him slightly on his arm, Storm continued to call him. "Luck, babe... get up and get in the bed."

Stirring awake, he looked at her with squinted eyes. Throwing his arm over his eyes to block out the light from the bay windows that adorned their living room, he mumbled that he was okay where he was.

"Get your ass up and get in the bed." Storm fussed, not accepting his answer. Just then, Steven answered his phone.

"*Wassup?*" He asked, sounding like he, himself was still in bed.

"*You cheatin' on your wife, nigga?*" Storm asked, not bothering for the fake chit chat that was sure to take place. Luck's arm flew from over his face as he looked up at Storm.

"*What the fuck are you talking about?*" Steven asked, wide awake now.

"*Your wife called me a little while ago and told me that you're up to your old ways again. I'm just gonna tell you now, don't lose your family fucking around with these mashed potatoes and shit.*"

"Mashed potatoes?" Lucky and Steven repeated after her at the same time.

"*Yeah,*" she responded to them both. "*Them side pieces... mashed potatoes, corn, beans... whatever the fuck you wanna call them.*"

Cracking up laughing, Luck sat up on the couch and shook his head. "*You're crazy as fuck.*"

"*Storm, don't listen to Amber's insecure ass... ain't no one cheatin' on her.*"

"*Don't do that, especially not with me on the phone. If she's insecure, it's because you made her that way with all the bullshit you put her through. But if Lucky's ass walked in this house at two in the morning and his first stop was the bathroom to wash off his dick, he wouldn't have one. So, no... it's not her being insecure. It's you doing shit you know better than doing.*"

"*Don't put me in that shit. You're it for me... I ain't stupid.*"

"Say that shit, baby!" Storm turned to Luck with a smile on her face before turning back around and paying attention to her phone. *"Have you heard The Carters new album, 'Everything is Love'?"*

"Man, fuck them and their new album. That ain't got shit to do with my life." Steven exclaimed.

"Yeah iight, you can say that now, but you better take heed. They talk about some shit on that album that clearly you need to hear. You keep it up if you want but you'll be okay when you're sitting your ass up in that house by your lonesome."

With that, Storm hung up the phone on Steven and went to the kitchen to grab everything she needed for her stay in bed before making her way upstairs with Luck trailing behind her.

2

"ONE STEP AWAY..."

-Tammy Rivera

"**W**hat's today's schedule like, babe?" Lucky asked Storm after they had dropped Lauryn off to school. It was rare that the two of them were able to drop her off to school together in the morning, so when they could, they made sure to do so. Under normal circumstances, that was a task for Storm being that Luck's days started really early or ended really late most days.

"You have a meeting with the label at 11 to discuss your album, an interview and photoshoot with New Era at one-thirty, they're going to follow you around for a few hours today. Then a meeting at five-thirty with Mona Scott for the reality show she's pitching. Afterwards, you have some studio time booked but that's about it."

"For real? That's all?"

"Yep..."

"I haven't had a light day like this in forever..." the excitement was evident in his voice. "You want to go get some breakfast?"

"Sure," Storm smiled at him from the passenger's seat while he drove to their destination. The whole ride there, silence engulfed the two of them. Storm could only imagine what was going through Luck's mind while she contemplated how she would bring up the conversation about getting her tubes tied once again.

After twenty minutes, they had arrived at the restaurant, were seated, and handed their menus before being given some privacy.

"What's on your mind?" Luck asked before she could even get her jacket off or get comfortable in the booth that they were seated in.

"What makes you think something is on my mind?"

"I know you like the back of my hand... there's something on your mind. You were quiet the whole way here, that's unheard of." He chuckled which resulted in Stormie rolling her eyes.

"I do not talk a lot." She protested.

"Yeah, whatever you say. Now spill the beans."

Hesitating momentarily, she decided to just blurt it out. "We need to talk about me getting my tubes tied, Luck. I've given it a lot of thought... I really have and I think that me getting my tubes tied is the best option. I've been battling depression for years now behind not being able to carry another baby. I don't want to feel like this anymore. I'm so miserable, Luck." Taking a minute to pull herself together, she quickly swiped the stray tears from her cheeks and continued with her plight. "I know you want more kids, and I do too... so, I looked into adoption. We just have to complete a few classes, get licensed, and have the social workers..."

Holding his hand up to stop her from continuing with what she was saying, Storm braced herself for whatever he was about to say. "Hell no. Hell no. Hell fucking no. We are not adopting, not when we are perfectly capable of having our own children. I get it, it's hurtful when we find out we're pregnant and then something goes wrong. Trust me, I know, Storm. I feel that shit too, only I can't let my emotions out because I gotta be there for you. I gotta make sure you aren't losing it, but that doesn't mean that I'm not hurting too. I'm suffering with you, Stormie but I know our suffering isn't in vain. Ain't no way we going through all of this if there isn't a pot of gold at the end of the rainbow and as long as it's the two of us together, I'm willing to go through whatever to get to the pot of gold." Reaching across the table to wipe that tears that were continuously falling from her eyes, Luck let his hand linger on her cheek for a while before grabbing Storm's hand. "We are in this together, baby. I know it's been difficult but that has never stopped us before. Just don't give up, you're too strong and determined for that. Okay?"

Even though she wanted to agree with everything that he had said, there was no way that she could. The truth was, that continuing to try to have a baby would break her... mind, heart, and spirit if her outcome was anything like it had been previously. "I can't, Luciano. I feel like I'm losing my mind." Storm told him in a pained whisper, tears further clouding her vision. The pain that she was feeling in that moment was enough to cripple her for the rest of the year.

"Can't isn't a word and you know it. You can and you will."

"Luck..."

Raising his hand, he shook his head to let her know that he didn't want to talk about it anymore. She knew that it would have been pointless to continue to go against the grain at this moment. They were out at breakfast... the last thing she wanted to do was cause a scene in this restaurant and have their business all up in the blogs.

Luck was clearly not changing his mind at this moment. There were no questions being asked in what he had just said, he was telling her what was going to happen, not asking her what she wanted to happen just like she hadn't asked him what he wanted. She would just have to revisit this conversation in the next couple of weeks with a different approach.

"HEY LALA! You're looking good, girl." Stormie smiled at Lucky's receptionist. She loved that woman; when she was hired, Lala was fresh out of college and that was three years ago. Unbeknownst to her, she was about to get promoted, but Luck and Storm were having a hard time finding someone to replace her. Therefore, she was still his receptionist for the moment.

"Thank you, you're lookin' damn good yourself." She returned the compliment back to Storm.

"Flattery will get you everywhere." Storm joked with her as she and Luck headed back to the conference room where Luck's meeting would be held.

"Y'all act like I'm not standing here... shit, if it wasn't for me, Storm wouldn't look like shit." Luck joked causing Storm to hit him upside his head.

"You're a damn lie!" Storm exclaimed.

"You iight," Lala called out to Luck's backs.

With everything that Storm and Luck had been going through with trying to conceive a new baby, the miscarriages, and the heartbreak, Storm felt it was best that she hired help. She had been Luck's manager and personal assistant since she had graduated college all of those years ago, but she couldn't do it all on her own anymore. Hence the promotion that Lala would be getting.

Storm would still be his manager, but Lala was gonna be his

personal assistant. Storm couldn't wait for her to take over because she was running herself thin doing it all.

Three hours later, the couple was leaving the office hand in hand with smiles on their faces. Luck's singles had been chosen, a release date had been set, his music video concept for his first single had been discussed, his photo shoot for his album as well as filming days, and more.

Luck was more than excited with the turn out of this meeting. He had been working on this album for the past two years, writing, erasing, recording, re-recording, mastering songs, and then remastering them. He couldn't figure out what was the most important message that he wanted to convey.

With over a hundred songs completed, he had narrowed the song list to eighteen songs and was still thinking about adding in another song or two before it was released for good. Out of all of the songs on his album though, there was one that was his favorite. One that even Storm hadn't heard. It described everything that Storm had been and still was to him. He couldn't wait for her to hear the song; he was sure she would love it just as he did.

"Where are you at on finding Lala's replacement? I'm ready to step down..." Storm asked as soon as they were back in the car.

"You don't wanna be with me all the time anymore?"

"You know I do... but I'm worn out. Look at these bags under my damn eyes!" She complained, pulling down the sun visor so that she could have access to the mirror.

"You look good to me. I don't see no bags."

"You don't see these double stuffed grocery bags sitting on my face?!"

Laughing, Luck shook his head while starting the car. "You're a damn fool, you know that?"

"I take it you notice the bags now, huh?" Storm asked as she laughed along with Luck.

After he had pulled off, he finally gave her the answer to her question. "Someone referred this guy to me, I wanted to interview him and possibly hire him without you knowing to surprise you, but you might as well be there because if he's not up to par, you'll be stuck finding the replacement again."

"So, when are we interviewing him?" Excitement coursed through her veins at not having to work so much.

"I'll give you his information when we make it back in the house later. You can call him and set it up tomorrow."

"Or, I can do it tonight."

"Whatever floats your boat." He told her, turning his music up and pressing his foot on the gas.

"Daddy!!" Lauryn screamed, dropping everything she had been working on just seconds earlier to run to her father. Crossing her arms over her chest and pouting, Storm watched all of the love that Lau gave her father before feigning jealousy.

"I don't get this kind of welcome when I come to pick you up..." Storm said, poking at Lauryn's side causing her to buckle and laugh.

"You pick me up every day, mommy."

"Wow!"

Getting down from Luck's arms, Lauryn ran to her mother and wrapped her arms around her legs. "I'm sorry, mommy!"

"No you're not, but it's okay baby." Leaning down to give Lauryn a hug, Storm released her and told her to grab her bag.

The second Lauryn had her bag in hand, she was once again running full force towards Lucky who was standing at the door to her classroom holding it open.

"Where are we going?" Lau asked, as she climbed in the back-seat of Luck's car.

"Home, girlfriend." Storm told her, immediately putting a frown on Lauryn's face.

"Where you wanna go?" Luck asked, after he was in the car with the door closed.

"Home." Storm said, turning to Luck with a raised eyebrow.

"No, can we go to World On Wheels?" Lauryn spoke up, already knowing her father would say yes.

"You think you can out skate me?" Looking back at Lauryn with a smile on his face, he completely ignored Storm. Storm wanted nothing more than to go home, wash the day off of her, and climb in bed but she could already see that the rest of her day wasn't going to happen that way. Lauryn had Luck wrapped around her finger and if she wanted to go skating, Storm could bet her last dollar that they were going skating.

"Uh huh," Smiling her toothless smile, Lauryn violently shook her head.

"Well, we're gonna find out." Turning around in his seat, Luck pulled his seatbelt across him and secured it before he started the car and pulled out of the parking lot.

"What locker number do you want?" Storm asked Luck as he took off his sneakers and replaced them with skates.

"Don't matter."

"This one, mommy!" Lauryn shouted over the loud music, showing the locker she had chosen for the three of them.

Skating over to where Lauryn was standing, holding the locker open, Storm stuffed all of their belongings into it before feeding it her quarters.

"You ready?" Already, Luck was struggling in his skates making Storm laugh. "Are you sure you're up to this?"

"I got this man. Y'all go ahead. I'll meet y'all." Laughing, Storm took heed to his words. She grabbed Lauryn's hand and they skated off to the floor.

Two hours later, Lauryn and Storm were worn out and Luck's knees were pained and bruised. He had fallen more than he could remember while trying to keep up with Lauryn making him regret even agreeing to go skating.

"We're never doing this again..." Luck said the second they were in the car and situated. Storm was sitting in the driver's seat and Luck was in the passenger's seat. There was no way he could drive with his knees on fire the way they were.

Laughing, Storm shook her head before pulling off into traffic. "It wasn't that bad; I actually had a really good time."

"Yeah, you would say that." Luck fussed, putting his seat back to stretch out a bit more. "That shit was horrible. All those old heads skating like they the only ones on the damn floor and shit. Got my baby scared to skate around the damn..."

"You better not!" Storm laughed, cutting her eyes at Luck. "Don't you blame my baby for your none skating ways. She had a blast; it was you that was struggling."

Bursting out laughing, she put her focus back on the road. Lucky wanted to laugh with her, instead he sucked his teeth before putting his arm over his eyes and mumbling 'yeah, whatever.'

"What are we eating for dinner?" It was already after 6 which put a damper in Storm's original plans to make beef ribs, mac and cheese, and kale.

"I thought you were cooking?"

"Yeah, that was the plan before your ass decided we were having family day on a Wednesday."

"Come on, man... I been looking forward to dinner all day."

"Well unless you're planning on eating at midnight, you're out of luck."

"I was planning on eating at midnight too." Luck said, raising his arm and peeking at Storm with a smirk on his face.

Looking into the rearview mirror to make sure that Lauryn was asleep, Storm glanced over at Luck with a smirk on her face as well.

"Oh, I know you were. Shit, I been thinking about you eating at midnight all day."

The two of them carried on with their flirting the rest of the ride home. By the time Storm made it to their home, Luck had talked her into making a shrimp scampi for dinner and to give him a private dance later that night. It had been a week since the methotrexate shot and she had stopped bleeding two days ago. Her and Lucky were both ready to indulge in each other and thankfully, there was nothing stopping them from doing so.

"TELL ME WHY YOU GONE WHEN YOU SHOULD BE HERE..."

-Tammy Rivera

"*Guess who I saw yesterday!*" Amber couldn't wait to spill the beans, so before Storm even had a chance to guess who she had seen, she was telling her. *"Erin's ass, she moved back to New York!"*

Erin was Storm and Steven's first cousin. Their mother's only sibling's child. Erin, Storm and Steven had grown up as brothers and sisters. Back in the day, their mothers were inseparable which led to the three of them being inseparable as well. Before Erin's mother died, she would take Storm and Steven every other weekend to her house. There was always a fun night planned when she was involved.

The closeness remained even after Erin's mother killed herself, Erin's father and the woman he had been cheating on her with. Knowing that she was the next best thing to a mother to

Erin, Storm and Steven's mother, Pam took her in and raised her. From the time she was six years old until she was 17.

When her first love got killed and she found out that she was pregnant, Erin decided that New York wasn't for her anymore. Making the decision to move to Atlanta with her aunt from her dad's side, that's where she stayed for the past five years raising her daughter.

Storm and Steven tried to remain close with her, letting her know she wasn't alone by making surprise trips to Atlanta, sending money for clothes for her and Damia, her daughter. They constantly called her just to see how she and Mia were doing but Erin didn't want any parts. Not that she was upset with them, she was just upset with life and the cards she had been dealt. Her entire pregnancy was spent in bed with her depressed, it even carried on for a while after Damia was born. Finally, after a good tongue thrashing from various family members, Storm and Steven included, she snapped out of it.

Now, she was back, and Storm, Steven and Erin were excited that they would all be together again. Not to mention Amber as well. Finally, they could be the crutches that they all needed for each other once again.

"I knew that... I saw her when Luck and I did that pop up visit a little while ago."

"Wait, she been here that long and I'm just now finding out? Neither one of you bitches are shit..." Even though Storm couldn't see Am, she knew she was pouting. Amber hated to be left out of anything.

"No, she was in town looking for a place and going to see Dame's family. You know they didn't know anything about Damia all these years. The last time I saw her was when she was going to see them. I thought you knew... shit, Steven saw her."

"Well, you know how I feel about Steven, so we won't even go there.

But yeah, she told those people about Damia. Dame's sister put his hands on her, I almost went there and showed my ass... she's lucky Erin stopped me but if I ever see her ass in the street, it's on and popping." Rolling her eyes, Amber plopped down in her seat at her office. She had come into work early today for a nine o'clock appointment that never showed, so she had a bit of time to kill, hence her early morning call to Storm.

"Wait, what?! His sister played like that? She knows she don't want these problems." Storm said, frustrated that she didn't know anything about it. Feeling herself getting excited, she decided to switch gears in the conversation back to Steven. *"Did he say anything to you about my call to him?"* It had been a few days since Storm and Steven had their conversation. She was almost certain that he brought it up to Amber as a way to start conversation... that was his normal routine, at least.

"No, I haven't been seeing him much these past few days."

"Y'all live in the same house, how the hell have you not been seeing him?"

"I been avoiding his ass like the Ebola infected Romaine Lettuce. I come home early and be sleep before he makes it in, I sleep in the room with Autumn sometimes... hell, one night, I stayed at y'all mom's house."

"Wow, shit is really that bad between y'all?"

"You thought I was playing... I don't want that shit anymore."

"I thought it would get worked out, I didn't think it had gotten to this extreme."

"Well, now you know. I'm over it..."

"You aren't over it, y'all been together for all of these years, there is no way you can just be over it like that."

"That's what you think. I haven't had any outburst, cried any tears, or felt any sorrow in my heart over this. I guess I did enough of that throughout my relationship with him to be partaking in any of that now."

Realizing that there was nothing else to say, she shook her head and blew out a deep breath before carrying on with the conversation.

"Anyway, I need a vacation!" Storm whined to Amber... *"We need a girl's trip... I wanna be turned up like the cast of 'Girl's Trip'. Shit, maybe we should go to Essence Fest."*

"Girl, you do realize that was a movie? They were probably tired as hell and tired of each other on some of the funniest parts."

"Don't steal my joy, Amber!"

"Okay, okay... but I need a vacation too. Without the kids, we need something just for us ladies."

"Yes, Erin, you, and myself."

"That sounds like a plan. Let's put something together."

"Okay, I'm on it. I'll start looking into all this shit now so we can get the hell out of here. I'm letting you know now we not going no place unless it's a week or better."

"A whole week? Damn, that's long as hell Storm."

"What's the purpose of going on vacation if we're only gonna be there for a few days? I want to enjoy myself."

"You're right... my clients are gonna be pissed though."

"They'll be alright. Shit, you need a life too!"

"You right, you right. Alright... well just let me know when, where, and how much. I'll be there with bells on."

Excitement coursed through Stormie's body as she started mentally preparing herself for the vacation she was about to plan. They were gonna have enough fun to last them for many years to come, she was going to make sure of it.

"Yes! I'm gonna start working on it now. I'll have all of the information to you in the next few days. I'm gonna call Erin now and let her know."

"Alright, I'll talk to you later."

"Okay, love you, sis."

"Love you too."

"Yo, Storm." Luck yelled, damn near at the top of his lungs even though he was walking in the room where she was at already.

"Shit, Luck! You scared me!" Storm hadn't heard him come in nor come up the stairs, but here he was.

"What the fuck is this?" Storm knew what it was the second she looked at his hand. When Luck dropped it at the foot of the bed for her to look at, her heart dropped. Squinting her eyes, she pretended that she couldn't see what the paperwork was. Looking up at Luck, she gave him a questioning look before she reached over and grabbed the paperwork that he had dropped on the bed.

Taking much longer than necessary to read the papers, Luck just about lost it. "What the fuck is this, Storm?" He screamed, snatching the papers away from her and throwing them on the floor.

"My appointment papers," Storm all but whispered.

"Appointment papers? Appointment for what? Not the same appointment we agreed wouldn't happen."

"*We* didn't agree on anything, you spoke, I listened... I didn't agree."

"You didn't agree?!" Luck was so upset spit was flying from his mouth. Being that he was standing over Storm, it was showering her, but she refused to move. The last thing she wanted to do was make this situation worse in anyway. "What the fuck didn't you agree with? Huh?"

"First of all, Luck, I'm not your child. Don't curse at me and talk to me like you're scolding me. I'm your wife... talk to me like you have some sense." Looking up at Luck, she waited to see if he would have a response for her even though she knew he would.

"If you weren't acting like a fucking child, this wouldn't be a problem."

Getting infuriated, Storm stood up from her place on the bed forcing Luck to back up a little bit. "Acting like a child? How dare you! I'm acting like a child because I want to have surgery to tie my tubes? It's my body!! I can do what I please with my body! You had the nerve to call me selfish when I brought it to you the first time but that's bullshit. I have unselfishly given my body to our plight to have another child. I've been pregnant more times than I can count on one hand. Each and every time, it has ended the same way with the exception of Lauryn and she wasn't even planned! If anyone is being selfish, it's you! You aren't even trying to understand what the hell I'm feeling right now. All you care about is you wanting to have another child. You wouldn't be able to walk half a mile in my shoes! Fuck you and your one-sided opinion. You couldn't begin to understand what the fuck I'm experiencing."

"You know what..." Luck stared at Storm like he wasn't sure if he wanted to say what was on his mind yet or not.

Seeing that he was struggling with whatever was on his mind, Storm butt in. "Nah, I don't know."

"Fuck this shit... you wanna do what you want to do. Clearly what the fuck I'm saying isn't important to you because if it was, this wouldn't be a conversation we were having for the third time. So, you're free to do as you please. I'm out." Spinning around, Luck damn near ran out of the room leaving Storm standing in the same spot with a confused look on her face.

What the fuck just happened?

There was no way Luck was that pissed that he would walk out on her, right? Unbeknownst to her, Luck was asking what the fuck had just happened as well. He couldn't even begin to phantom the fact that he had just walked out on his wife, but the act had already been done. His pride wouldn't allow him to go back in the house and make amends as fucked up as it was.

Climbing in his truck, he started his car and pulled off without ever once looking up at his bedroom window where Storm was standing watching in disbelief.

"It's been a whole week since I've seen he's been gone, E. He hasn't called or checked in with me."

"He hasn't even called for Lauryn?"

"He pops up at her school randomly throughout the day... but still."

"I know..." Storm and Erin had been on the phone for the past hour talking about everything going on in her household. *"I don't really know what else to suggest, Stormie. He isn't answering any number associated to you, he's not using his credit cards or debit cards knowing you have access to them. The only thing I can say is wait it out... he's not leaving you. You could try to kill that man and he would still hold it down. He loves you."*

"Maybe that's not enough... I don't see my mind changing on wanting to get this tubal litigation. There are other options but, in his stubbornness, he's not even trying to hear that."

"Just like in your stubbornness you aren't trying to hear what he has to say either."

"Touche."

"I just want the both of you to sit down and have a heart to heart... a real heart to heart where you both are listening to understand and not just to respond. I don't know if it will help, but at least the two of you will know where you both stand and possibly you can find a medium."

"Well, that's not possible if he isn't here. I didn't run... he did. I was here for a conversation the whole time. He just wanted to dictate though."

"Bullshit!" Luck spoke up, finally deciding to make his presence known. He had been standing in the doorway of their bedroom watching Storm lay on her side while she talked to Erin for the past ten minutes.

Snapping her head back so that she could see Luck, her face showed every emotion she was feeling at that moment. Uncertainty, anger, sadness, frustration... she couldn't pinpoint one emotion, and neither could Luck.

"Can we talk?" He asked, still not moving from the spot he was standing in. For some crazy reason, he was waiting on a warm welcome from Stormie that he wouldn't receive.

"Now you wanna talk?" The venom dripped from her words. Now that he was back, her missing him had dissipated and anger had replaced it. One could say she was scorned to an extent... there was no way a conversation between the two of them should have resulted in him running away from home.

"Storm!" Erin shouted through the phone that was still on speaker. "Let him speak... hell you both need to speak *and listen!* Talk to him and I'll talk to you later."

Not waiting for Storm to respond, Erin hung up leaving Storm and Luck their privacy.

After seven days of not showing his face in their home, Luck was standing there watching her with those funny colored eyes that she loved and hated at the same time. Storm wanted to curse him out, tell him to go back to wherever the hell he came from, shit, she even wanted to put hands on him. However, the truth was that she had missed him, but that didn't mean she was going to be easy on him.

"Storm..."

Raising her hand, she silenced him. "I don't want any apologies... I get it. We're facing a hard time and I get it but you aren't the only one going through it. We don't have to always agree with each other but leaving isn't an option, Lucky. So, you left this time, that was your one... you used it. Next time, you'll be coming home to an empty house. Got it?" Staring at him, she could see the smirk playing on his face that he was trying to conceal, desperately. He loved when she bossed up on him...

"You're right and even though you said you don't want an apology; I owe you one. So, I want to start by apologizing. I shouldn't have left like that... hell, I shouldn't have left at all if I'm being honest."

"You sure shouldn't have..." Storm said continuing to give him a hard time.

"I said that already, Storm. I also apologized for that. My emotions got the best of me and I reacted based off of that. However, what I said still stands... if you get that surgery, I'm done. I love you with everything in me, but that's something I don't think I'll be able to get over. You aren't even trying to find out what's going on with your body. Get some test done, figure out what we can do... change our diets, do in vitro, pray, see specialist. One of the main purposes of marriage and unions is to reproduce and bear children, I want more children, Storm. Not adopted children, children that come from me and from you. I want to see who we create. Lauryn is an amazing child; she's funny, beautiful, smart, caring and the perfect blend of us... and she came from us. Don't you want to see who else we create?" Luck asked, tears in his eyes as he pleaded his case to his wife.

With tears in her eyes, Storm understood exactly what he was saying and where he was coming from. She just couldn't see herself going through the plight of trying to have more children again. However, she wasn't going to tell Luck that. "I do want to see who else we create. Can't you tell? We've been trying for years to create more little beings. I just don't know what else to do." She wasn't lying... she really didn't know what else to do which is why she wanted to just get the surgery and call it a day.

"Well, can we find out together?"

Shaking her head, she agreed with him. For now, she would try things his way. She was still going to set her appointment and if Luck and her couldn't find another way before then, she was going through with it.

"Yo, STORM WHERE YOU AT?" Luck asked as soon as he walked through their front door.

"We're in here, daddy!" Lauryn responded to him before Storm had a chance to answer him.

"Thanks, Storm." Stormie sarcastically said to Lauryn who was getting her hair braided. Thankfully, Storm had only two braids left because she was tired of the whining Lauryn was carrying on with.

Laughing, Lau didn't bother responding to her mother as Storm started on a new braid, shutting Lauryn up in the process.

Walking in the living room, Luck smiled at the sight. Besides his mother, there was no one else in the world that he loved as much as he loved the two of them. Despite the shit that Storm and him were going through, he was proud of his life and his love with her. He couldn't picture this with anyone else.

"Hey beautiful," Luck said, purposely not addressing either woman directly.

"Hey, daddy."

"Hey, baby." Storm and Lau responded at the same time causing him to laugh.

"I think he was talking to me, little girl."

"No, he wasn't. You were talking to me, right daddy?"

"I was talking to you both," he responded, drawing a side eye from Storm.

"How was the meeting?" Storm asked, with her attention still focused on Lauryn's head.

"It went alright... not exactly the way that I thought it would have gone but it could have gone worse so I'm not gonna complain."

"I feel you... I'm sorry it didn't work out the way you thought it would but like you said, it could have gone worse, so that's always good."

"Right, anyway what you have planned for the night? Do you wanna go with me to Rick and Melia house tonight?"

"Why, what they got going on?" Storm was dying to get out of the house today. Besides going to get Lau from school or running to meetings and studio sessions with Luck, she didn't do much. Most of her outings were work related, and Storm couldn't complain about that. On Tuesdays, Luck and her did industry night at Pinz with the rest of the industry cats and there was always a party or an industry event for them to attend, but she couldn't let her hair down at those places.

"They're having a game night tonight."

"Oh, that sounds like fun... I definitely wanna go."

"Good, cuz they are talking shit about how we're gonna get our asses beat in spades by them."

"They must not know." Storm chuckled.

"I tried to tell them."

"That's okay, we're gonna show them today."

"Can I come, daddy?" Lauryn asked from her space on the floor.

"Not this time, baby girl. This is for adults only." Luck told her before refocusing his attention on Storm. "I already called Kelsey to babysit Lau, so we're all set. We gonna head over there around 7 or 8 but we are going to grab some food before that."

"Okay, I see you... you're on point today." Storm laughed.

"Yeah, besides the fact that I wanted to show these niggas who was going to come out on top, I felt we needed this."

Smiling, Storm had to agree. With the constant bickering and fussing present between the two of them regarding the surgery and everything, they did need this time together.

"So, what time do you want to go and get food?"

"Kelsey is on her way now, so you can go and start getting ready. You don't have to get all dressed up babe, we just chilling today."

"That's what I like to hear." Storm joked with him, finishing the last braid in Lauryn's head, she jumped up and headed straight to the shower.

An hour and a half later, the two of them were on their way to get some food. Dressed in a pair of Nike leggings, an oversized off the shoulder tee and a pair of Huarache's, Storm was expecting to eat in the car. Unfortunately, that wouldn't be the case. Luck's stardom afforded him the opportunity to shut places down, but today, he just wanted to be regular with his wife. Even though he was living his dreams and was happy about that, he missed the simplicity of just being himself.

Pulling up to Providence, he drew a crazed look from Storm. "I know you didn't bring me here after telling me that I didn't need to get dressed up."

"Storm, I'm dressed down, just like you. So, cut it out and let's go." Luck told her, referring to his Off White sweatpants and tee shirt. On his feet were a pair of NMD's that he had only worn once before.

Pouting, Storm got out of the car when valet opened her door and found her place next to Luck. Hand in hand, the two of them made their way into the restaurant. Storm was a lover of seafood and with that in mind, Luck made reservations for the two of them at this restaurant.

"Luciano Johnson," Luck told the hostess as they approached the podium that she was stationed behind.

Storm and Luck laughed amongst themselves as the hostess got herself together. Clearly, she was starstruck and having a hard time formulating her words and body movements. After dropping the menus and the utensils they would be using more then twice, Luck decided to help her. Grabbing a menu for himself and Storm, as well as utensils, he then waited on the hostess to show them to their seats.

"I am so sorry." She apologized profusely as rubbed her hands down her skirt.

"No problem at all... he's used to it." Storm told her, smiling to help her calm down a bit.

Once they had been escorted to their seats, Storm wasted no time picking up her menu. After she had figured out what she wanted, she looked up and saw Luck staring at her.

"What?"

"You hungry hungry, huh?" He joked, causing Storm to erupt in laughter.

"Shut up, stupid..."

"I'm just saying. Your stomach is over there talking other languages and shit. I swear it just said some shit in Arabic." Laughing at his silliness, Storm had to admit that her stomach was doing the most right now.

"I wasn't this hungry until I got in here, but yeah... I'm hungry, hungry."

"What you getting?" He asked, already knowing what he wanted.

"I want oysters to start and the black cod for my main course. I want dessert too, but I'll wait until I finish eating to get that."

"Damn, I thought you were gonna be a cheap date."

"Ain't shit cheap about me, boo. You know that."

"You better be ready to bust that shit open tonight."

"Oh, so because you spend a few dollars on me you think I'm gonna have sex with you? Who do you think I am?" Storm asked, pretending as if she had taken offense to what Luck had just said.

Truth was though, this was their norm. They got a kick out of causing small scenes and playing around in public. They always seemed to get a rise out of people until they realized that they were playing and then everyone would join in on the laugh. Sometimes, people wouldn't intervene at all, simply watch on while others would break their necks to stop whatever they thought was going on.

Their joking came to an end when their waitress made her way to their table. Although she was dressed in the standard attire that the other waitresses and waiters were in, hers was extra provocative. Her shirt hung low in the front, showing all but her nipples. The black skirt that she had on was exposing her to the world. Although she was fully covered, she was still naked.

With really dark skin, full lips, big almond shaped eyes, and a pointed nose, Storm had to give the woman her props. She was a beauty.

"Hi, my name is Mel, I'll be your waitress today. What drinks can I start you all with?" She asked, with her attention only on Lucky.

Sitting back in her seat, Storm had to laugh. Had she been the same person she was a few years ago, she would have taken offense to the public disrespect this woman was displaying. At this day and age though, there wasn't much that could ruffle her feathers when it came to her husband and other women. Storm would bet her last dollar on Luck and his faithfulness and loyalty to their union.

"Baby, what you want?" Luck asked, with his attention focused on Storm.

"Bring us a bottle of your best wine please." Storm told her, still looking at the back of the woman's head.

Noticing that she hadn't written anything down, Luck took his attention off of Storm and looked up at the waitress. "Did you hear my wife?"

"Oh yes, I'm sorry." She said scribbling in the pad she was holding. "I'll be right back with that."

"No, wait." Storm stopped her, picking up her and Luck's menu. "We're ready to order."

Looking as if it pained her to put her attention on Storm, she turned around and looked at Storm, giving her, her undivided attention. After rambling off her selection, she proceeded to give Luck's order as well. Once again, the young lady didn't write down anything that Storm had said, but this time, neither Storm nor Luck commented on it. When she had walked away, Storm looked up at Luck getting ready to say what was on her mind. Before she could utter the words, Luck was saying it.

"She better not fuck up neither one of our orders either."

"You know me so well." Storm laughed.

"I feel like I haven't heard you laugh this much in months." Luck admitted. A part of him felt bad about the fact that Storm wasn't happy 24/7. In his mind, as her husband he was supposed to do any and everything he could to see her in this state and lately, he hadn't known what to do to get her to smile.

"It has been a long time, huh?"

"Yeah man... I missed this playful and light side of you. Shit been hectic with us for a while."

"It has, but everyone goes through things... it's about how we get through them."

"Yeah, but I don't really know how we're supposed to get through this. Shit's been different."

"We get through it the same way we been getting through it

Lucky. We deal with it... not run from it. Running from it won't change anything because when you return, that problem is going to still be there and by then, it will have festered for so long that it'll be even bigger than it was before."

"I didn't think about it like that."

"That's why I'm your better half," smiling, Storm reached across the table to grab Luck's hand before giving it a light squeeze.

"You know that if I could take on the shit you dealing with, I would do it in a heartbeat right? Like, if I could carry the rest of our children or go through even half of the shit you been going through and conquering I would without a second thought."

"I know, Luck. Trust me, I know. But all I need from you is for you to be there with me and be understanding. Don't be so quick to shut down my ideas and thoughts without even giving it a chance. Just like you, I'm trying to find solutions and ways to better our situation."

"I know, and I'm sorry if I've come off as insensitive or even controlling. I've noticed that I've had a 'my way or the highway' approach lately and I apologize. Your opinion and feelings are just as important as mine are if not more important. I just don't know how to deal with this shit."

"Together, Luck... that's the only way. I can't do this without you."

"And you don't have to." Luck promised her, and she believed him.

"COME TAKE A SHOWER WITH ME." Storm was already in bed, buried under the covers and half dead to the world, but the minute she heard Luck's voice, she was wide awake. Game night had been a success, but Storm had drunk just a bit too much. So,

41

while Luck was downstairs on the phone, Storm made her way upstairs and in the bed.

With all the arguing and fussing they had been doing lately, things had been hectic between the two of them and Storm was missing him.

Getting up from the bed, she went to their shared dresser and pulled it out to get them some underclothes. "You can leave all of that shit right there."

Looking up from what she was doing, she looked at Lucky with a questioning look.

"Ain't no clothes in the bed tonight."

Smirking, Storm put everything that was in her hands back in the draw while shaking her head up and down.

"I'm going to go run the water." Walking past Lucky, she pulled the oversized t-shirt she had been draped in over her head. Making it to the bathroom, she started the shower water before taking a seat on the toilet to release her bladder. After she was finished, she flushed the toilet and stepped in the shower.

Deciding to get a start on things, she grabbed the removable shower head. Positioning it so that the water stream was directly on her clit, she spread her legs and prepared herself for the pleasure that was sure to come.

"Shit," she hissed as the water sprayed with intensity on her most sensitive part.

"You started without me?" Lucky feigned hurt. His presence heightened what she was feeling at the moment. Her stomach tensed and the toes on her right foot curled before her head fell back and her mouth opened.

"Ahh shit," escaped her mouth as her orgasm came as a force to be reckoned with,

Luck stood in the same spot watching her with lust present in her face. "Is it my turn yet?" he inquired.

Instead of verbally responding to him, Storm made her way to him until she was invading his personal space. Getting down on her knees, she grabbed his hardened member and moved her hands down the length of it. Putting the head in her mouth, Storm used her teeth to apply pressure before opening wide and pushing his dick to the back of her throat. Gagging, she pulled back before shoving his dick down her throat once again. Using her free hand, she massaged his balls. A soft moan left Luck's lips before his hand found its way to her head. Taking control of the situation, he moved her head back and forth by pulling and pushing on her head.

Luck had encountered plenty of women in his life but no one had ever been able to do the things that Storm was able to do with her mouth. He hated to think about who had taught her to do all the shit with her mouth that he loved, but he was thankful for them. Storm was a fucking beast when it came to giving head and he appreciated it.

"Just like that, baby." Luck encouraged Storm, giving her the boost needed to take things to the next level. Pulling his dick from her mouth, the excess saliva trickled down her chin before she found herself replacing her hands on his balls with her mouth.

"Sss," he hissed, tightening the grip he had on her hair. Staring up at him, she saw the admiration for her in his eyes among other things. Having enough, he pulled Storm from her place on her knees and turned her around so that she was facing the wall. Placing her hands on the wall, he adjusted her so that she was positioned the way he needed her to be before he took his time inserting his member into her warm and silky cave.

"Oh, that feels so fucking good," She whispered, trying to get in line with his movements. Luck moved his hands to her waist, controlling her movements. Leaning forward, his teeth dug into her should, making her cream instantly. "Oh, Luck... yesss." She purred.

"Damn, this shit wet as fuck." He said, more to himself continuously pumping in and out of her with precision. As his climax approached, he sped up his pace, causing Storm to try to climb the wall. Storm didn't know what to do as it felt like Luck was trying to rip through her. She wanted to run but the pain was accompanied by a pleasure that she welcomed.

"Shit, don't move, Storm. Oh shit," he moaned. His fingers dug deep into her hips as he tensed, and she followed behind him. Seconds later, the two were releasing simultaneously. Kissing the back of her neck elicited a shiver from Storm. Pulling out of her, he turned her around before sensually kissing her.

"I love you," he told her.

With a smile on her face, Storm replied, "I love you more."

4

(3 MONTHS LATER) "... AND DON'T YOU REMEMBER THAT EVEN IF YOU WAS IN THE WRONG I STOOD BY YOUR SIDE?"

-Queen Naija

"What other options do I have?" Storm asked her GYN as the two of them sat in her office at the hospital. Today was supposed to be her surgery for the tubal ligation but at the last moment, she couldn't do it. All she could think about as she sat in the waiting room looking at the other women in there were Lucky's words to her when he came back home after his hiatus. During an argument one night, he told her *"If you do that shit, we're over, Storm... I mean that shit,"* and she believed him.

She didn't even get as far as running tests with the nurse before she was getting up and going to the receptionist to tell her that she had changed her mind. Requesting to speak to the doctor, she returned to her seat and got comfortable knowing it would be a wait. After forty-five minutes, her doctor finally called her back to talk to her.

"Well, there are all different kinds of fertility treatments that you can try out. There are surgeries, in vitro, fertility drugs... how about we schedule an appointment where your husband and you can both be present so that we can all discuss this together."

Blowing out a breath of frustration, Storm thanked her for her time before grabbing her belongings and leaving out of the hospital. The second she started the car, she sat back and stared at herself in the rearview mirror while thinking over her morning. After a few minutes, she turned her cell phone back on and waited for it to load. As soon as the screen returned to her lock screen, the alerts started going off. There were over fifty text messages from Lucky. Going to the text thread the two of them had, Storm frowned her face up in confusion as she read through the messages that he had sent her.

"What the fuck?" Leaving the message thread, she quickly went to her call log and called him as her heartbeat increased and her hands and underarms started to sweat.

"The number you have reached is no longer in service." Hanging up, thinking that maybe her phone had dialed something wrong even though his number and name was programmed in her phone, she went to the dial pad and dialed his number in.

Waiting for it to ring or him to answer, she was shocked when the same message came through the speaker again. Hanging up and Storm repeated the same process three more times before trying to call him from private and getting the same response. Her heart sank to the pit of my stomach as she realized that Luck had changed his number on her.

Speeding out of the hospital parking lot, she drove above the speed limit the whole way home. Storm needed to make this right, he was assuming right now, he needed to know the truth.

Not even bothering to close the gate to their house behind her or to cut her car off, she jumped out of the car and ran to her front door. Never even stopping to take a second to realize that Lucky's Jeep wasn't in the driveway, she ran full speed.

"Luck! Lucky!!" Storm screamed through the house as she ran through all the rooms trying to find him. After making it to the last room and still not finding him, everything she had been feeling at the moment broke inside of her and the waterfalls began.

Jogging back outside to her running car, she jumped back in and went to the next best place. Pulling up to the studio thirty minutes later, she sat there for a second trying to mentally compose myself. Storm ran over what she was going to tell him repeatedly in her head as she got out of the car and headed to the doors of the studio.

"Hi, Mrs. Johnson." Andrew, the security guard said the second Storm entered the building.

Smiling at him, she gave him a slight wave before heading to the elevators.

"Hey Lala," Stormie said with a smile on her face as she walked up to her desk.

"Hey Storm, what are you doing here today?"

"I came to surprise Lucky." Storm smiled, trying to hide all of the emotions inside of her.

Frowning, she looked up at her again. "He's not here."

Storm's face dropped, "he's not?"

"No, he hasn't been here all day."

"Oh..." Storm felt stupid. "Okay, well if he comes in later, let him know I was here."

"Is everything okay?" Stormie's eyes were getting cloudy again and she knew that if she didn't get out of there right away, she was going to embarrass herself.

"Yes," shaking her head up and down, she threw on a fake smile and backed away from the desk in the direction of the elevator. "Have a good day!" She told Lala with her back to her as she waited for the elevator doors to open. The walk back to the car was a long one, when Storm finally made it there, she didn't know what else to do with myself. Luck could have been at his best friend's house, but she would never bring our drama to their house.

Not sure what else to do, she rummaged through her pocket-book, looking for her phone but the tears that were brimming the rims of her eyes were preventing her from seeing. Growing frustrated, she turned her pocketbook upside down emptying the contents on the passenger's seat before grabbing her phone and calling Steven.

"Wassup, Chicken Little?" Had she not been so distraught in this moment, she would have probably smiled. That had been Steven's nickname for her since she was a child and she hadn't heard it in a long time, but it still warmed her heart.

"He left me." Storm was hysterical.

"Wait, calm down... I can't understand you."

"Lucky left me." she croaked out once she had calmed down just a little bit.

"What do you mean, he left you?"

"I mean he's gone; he's not home, he changed his number, he's not at the studio."

"You did that stupid ass surgery, Storm?!" Steven roared at her.

Shaking her head like he could see her, she finally verbally responded. *"No, I didn't. He thinks I did, but he didn't even give me a chance to explain anything to him."*

"Why does he think you did?"

"I was supposed to do the surgery today; I went in but couldn't go through with it. I'm supposed to go back with Luck so we can talk about

alternatives and treatments to help us have another baby. I don't even know how he knew that I was supposed to have the surgery today... I didn't tell him for this exact reason."

"Damn... don't you got to have your husbands consent for that surgery?"

"I'm not his child Steven, I'm his wife..."

"Some states require that shit."

"Well not California."

"Shit," Steven was clearly at a loss for words and this was the wrong time for it. Storm needed him to tell her what to do. She needed to figure out how she was going to contact Lucky so that she could make all of this right again.

"That's it? What should I do?"

"Give him time, Storm. He's not going to leave you, that nigga loves you... he just needs some time to cool off."

"There is nothing for him to cool off from. I didn't go through with the surgery. This is all just a misunderstanding."

"Had you not been sneaking around; this wouldn't even be the case. So, give him time, you owe him that." She wanted to argue with Steven, but that wouldn't do anything for her at the moment. Plus, her frustrations weren't with him, they were with Lucky and this messy ass situation they were in.

"If you hear from him just tell him to call me, please."

"I got you. If you need anything hit me up. I'll take off for a week and come spend some time with you."

"Thank you, I'll let you know." Hanging up, Storm decided to go and get Lauryn from school being that she knew that she wasn't leaving the house again once she made it in.

"Hi, Mrs. Johnson, you just missed your husband." Lauryn's teacher informed Storm, shocking the hell out of her. *I know this nigga ain't take my baby...*

"He was here?" Storm couldn't hide her shock. "Did he take Lauryn?" She could feel the heart attack coming even before she opened her mouth.

"No, she's here. He just brought her lunch and ate with her."

Sighing deeply, she silently thanked God before informing her teacher that she was signing her out early today. Minutes later, Lauryn's bubbly self was headed towards her looking nothing like what she looked like when she left the house this morning.

"Lauryn, what happened to your hair?" Storm questioned her as the two of them made their way out of her school.

"I don't know, Mommy."

Looking down at her, Storm shook her hand to get her attention before stopping and crouching down to her level. "You know what happened to your hair and you also know that Mommy doesn't like story telling..."

Storm could see the nervousness in her face as she contemplated whether she was going to tell her the truth or not. "Now, I'm going to ask you again, what happened to your hair? That's not how it looked when you left the house."

"Alyssa took out my braids. She said I looked prettier like this." Before Lauryn had left the house this morning, she had put two cornrows in her head, now it was out in a bushy mess.

"Didn't Mommy tell you not to let anyone touch or play in your hair?"

Shaking her head yes, Lauryn was still looking at the ground. Putting her hand under her chin, Storm lifted her head so that she would be looking at me. "I can't hear you, Lauryn, use your words."

"Yes."

"Okay, so how are we going to make sure that this never happens again?"

"I'm going to tell Alyssa that she can't play in my hair anymore."

"Good girl." Standing back up, the two of them headed to the car. Once they were in route home, she decided to ask Lauryn about Lucky bringing her lunch.

"So, Daddy brought you lunch today?"

"Yes, he brought me McDonald's. Look at my toy, Mommy." Peeking at her through the rearview mirror as she dug in the front of her book bag, Storm smiled. Seconds later, her hand returned holding a purple and pink toy.

"That's so pretty!" Storm cooed at her even though she had absolutely no idea what the toy was. A few seconds passed before she asked her the next question. The question she was dying to know the answer to.

"Did Daddy say what time he was coming home?" Storm felt pitiful as she waited for Lauryn to respond.

"No," she was so interested in her toy that Storm decided to leave her be. Then it was like she remembered something and spoke up after a few minutes had passed. "Daddy said he was going away for a while."

There was that roller coaster feeling again... "Away? Did he say where?"

"No, he didn't, Mommy."

Lost in her thoughts for the rest of the ride, Storm didn't know how she could fix this. However, Lucky had to at least talk to her in order for it to be fixable. With the way everything was right now, she would never be able to fix it. She had no way of reaching him. All she could do at this moment was bank on the fact that they would have to talk off of the strength of their baby. Lucky was a lot of things, but a deadbeat wasn't one of them. He would contact Storm eventually to check on Lau and she would use that to her advantage.

5

"I GAVE UP WHILE YOU HELD IT DOWN..."

-Mario

Two weeks...

Two whole weeks. That's how long it had been since Storm had seen or heard from Luck. She thought that by now, he would have come around but clearly that wasn't the case. Storm was an emotional wreck; she had tried everything she could think of to find Luck and talk to him, but he had stayed under the radar pretty well.

She had tried sliding in his DM's on Instagram and Snapchat, only to be left on seen. She had popped up at the studio and his office more times than she could count to find him never there. She had even broken down and went by his best friend's house to learn that he had never even went there. At this point, Storm had run out of ideas of where he could be.

"Hey Erin," Storm answered her ringing phone via the Blue-

tooth in her car. Today was Lau's last day of school so Storm was headed to get her a little early so they could have a girl's day.

"Hey Storm! Wassup? How are you feeling today?"

"The same as yesterday and the day before."

"Figures... that's why I was calling you."

"Wassup?" Storm asked, figuring that Erin was up to something.

"I think you should come to New York for a few weeks. You are sitting in that house all depressed and shit... I'm not feeling it. When Luck decides to come to his senses, he knows how to reach you. But you aren't about to sit in that house driving yourself mad behind him forgetting where his home is." Storm heard everything she said, but she was unsure if she wanted to leave her home. She wanted to be there when Luck finally did make it home.

"I don't know about that, E..."

"Storm, come on... you warned him already that if he left again you wouldn't be there, so what the hell are you sitting around waiting for?"

Thinking about what Erin said, Storm had to admit that she was right. Luck had been warned... if she stayed and he returned home, he would take her for a joke. *"You know what... you're right. I'll look for flights tonight."*

"I already took care of it. Your flight leaves tonight at 9:40 p.m. I just forwarded your itinerary to you."

"Tonight? How the hell do you expect me to pack for Lau and myself by tonight? That's only seven hours away, Erin... I'm not making that."

"Storm, max them fucking cards when you make it here..."

"Nah, we still married... his bills are my bills, bitch. But I will pull some cash out of this fucking safe."

"Now we're talking..."

"You going to come get me from the airport? Where the hell are we going to be staying?"

"Amber had a fit that I wanted you to stay with me, so, you know

how that goes. Therefore, either Am or Steven will be picking you up from the airport."

"Alright, I'll see you tonight... and thank you, E."

"You don't have to thank me, I love you."

"I love you too."

Hanging up the phone, Storm danced in her seat once she was done parking. Climbing out of the car, she had a smile on her face that hadn't been there in a few weeks.

She missed her family and maybe being there with them right now, while she was trying to deal with the bullshit with Lucky, would prove to be good for her and Lauryn as well.

Moments later, Storm and Lauryn were walking out of her school, hand in hand. Storm was still on cloud nine until Lauryn told her that Lucky had come to the school earlier that day. To make matters even worse, he had given her a cell phone for him to contact her.

Here it was Storm didn't even have a way of contacting Lucky being that he had changed his number, but he had given Lau a phone so that he could call her. Regardless of what the two of them were experiencing, they were adults with a child who still needed to communicate with each other for her sake.

That bit of information pushed Storm over the edge. She went from being sad to angry. Her mind was screaming fuck that nigga but her heart just wouldn't get on board. Storm had every mind to take the phone and when he called, she answered to force him to talk to her. However, the woman in her with dignity wouldn't allow her to.

Husband or not, there was only so much she would deal with... so much she could deal with. By now, her pride was bruised. If he didn't want to talk, Storm wouldn't make him. She just prayed he kept this same energy. If this was how Luck wanted to play, then he finally had a playing mate. Storm was done trying, she was forcing herself to be done.

"*Where are you, Amber?*" Storm fussed in her phone while she and Lauryn stood along the curb of the loading area.

Their flight had landed over an hour ago and after waiting damn near an hour for their bags to finally grace the carousel, Storm was frustrated. To top it off, she had to stand here and wait for slow ass Amber.

"*I'm coming around the bend now with your impatient ass.*"

"*My flight landed an hour and a half ago Amber... you should have been here ten times already. This don't make no damn sense. Got my baby and I standing here looking like fucking hobos with all these damn bags and shit.*"

Instead of waiting for a response, Storm disconnected the call and started gathering all the bags in her hand so that they could jump in and keep it moving.

As soon as Storm fixated her sight on Ambers car, she was moving towards it. The flight had been long and not the best if she could say. There was a dog on the flight directly in front of her which had her allergies cutting up the entire time, not to mention there was a baby across the aisle from her that just would not stop crying. Even with headphones in her ears, Storm couldn't relax to save her life.

Then to make matters worse, about halfway through the flight, there was horrible turbulence, and someone had a seizure right in the middle of the aisle. Storm had never witnessed a flight as bad as the one she had today and if she could help it, she never would again.

Flying private had spoiled her beyond belief and now she couldn't see herself ever reverting back.

"Damn, who pissed in your Cheerios today?" Amber asked like Storm didn't have a reason to be mad with her for her lateness alone.

"Hi Auntie Am!" Lauryn exclaimed once she had climbed in the car. Leaning over the console, she gave Amber a hug and kiss before Storm jumped in the passenger's seat and started barking orders.

"Lau, get your seatbelt on and Am, let's go with your late ass."

"Well, hey sis! I missed you too. You look... terrible, girl. Your eyes are swollen." Amber sarcastically said as she pulled away from the curb.

"Fuck you... but had you been on time, you could have gotten all of the hey sissy's in the world, but now... you can kiss my A double hockey sticks."

"Ohh, I know what you said mommy." Lauryn blurted from the backseat causing Amber and Storm to look at each other and burst out laughing.

"Mind your business, little girl. You don't know nothing." Storm told Lauryn while still laughing.

"I'm so glad you're back... even if it is only for two weeks. Talking on the phone don't have nothing on being able to actually see you and spend time with you."

"I'm glad to be back as well. I didn't know how much I needed this until Erin called me."

"I feel you, shoot... I need to get away also. I'm two seconds short from going to jail for murder."

Even though Amber laughed when she said it, Storm knew that it was far from a laughing matter. Although Amber hasn't been calling and telling Storm everything due to her situation with Lucky, she was still telling her some things. Storm had to admit that had she been in Amber's shoes, she would have pulled a Lorena Bobbitt already.

"Well, the girl's trip is still a go, right?"

"I thought that with everything going on right now with you and Luck you wouldn't want to do it."

"Truthfully, I don't want to do it, but I also don't want to mope around while he's out doing only God knows what."

"Oh please, you know that wherever Lucky is, he's on his best behavior. He's a lot of things but stupid isn't one of them."

"I sure hope you're right..." With Luck staying away as long as he had, Storm wasn't sure what to believe at this point and time. Luck was making Storm doubt a lot... from her relationship, him, and even herself.

"I am... but on to a brighter subject, did you bring some party attire?"

"Party attire for what? I came to relax, not turn up."

"Blah, blah, blah... the turn up is a part of the relaxation. Get some drinks in you and a good atmosphere and you'll be brand new talking about Luck who." Amber joked.

"The lies you tell. I will never be that drunk where I'm forgetting my husband, besides I don't even drink liquor anymore... only wine."

"Well, we are going to have to change that tonight."

Rolling her eyes, Storm saw that there wasn't much of a choice. Clearly, Amber and Erin had worked this out with each other without letting Storm know a thing. Even though Storm would have preferred to cuddle in bed with Lauryn and Autumn, she had to admit that a lady's night sounded much better.

"Where y'all heifers want to go anyway?"

"They have this new spot on Fulton and Bedford that I've been dying to get into. The music is always good when I pass by and the people be in there in crowds, so it has to be good."

"Or just like you, people could be feigning to get into somewhere new."

"Whatever you say, but we are going there tonight." Rolling her eyes, Storm sat back in her seat and grabbed her phone. In the background, Amber and Lauryn talked while Storm scrolled through her Instagram feed.

For the first time in two weeks, Luck had posted a picture of himself. It wasn't a full body picture, just one where she could see the top of his body. Dressed in a black hoody, and a burgundy and black dad hat, with minimal jewelry. There was no smile on his face and Storm could see the stress lines on his forehead and at the corners of his eyes. The bags and dark rings around his eyes told that he hadn't gotten much sleep in the past few days and his complexion was a bit blotchy. He was sitting in the studio with an up and coming artist, Kai Ca$h and the caption told Storm and the rest of the world that the two of them were working on a project.

Seeing him in the picture warmed Storm's heart. For whatever reason, she was under the impression that he was living his best life while the two of them were apart but seeing the state that he was currently in told her another story. Just like her, he was having a hard time coming to terms with the separation between the two of them.

"What are you looking at over there?" Amber interrupted Storm's thoughts.

"Nothing much," locking her screen, she placed her phone face down in her lap and talked to Am for the rest of the ride back to her house.

"WELCOME BACK TO NEW YORK, SIS!" Steven greeted Storm at the passenger door. Pulling the door open to gain access to her, he pulled her out of the car and closed her in his arms. He could only imagine how much she needed that hug, even with things rocky between Amber and him, he would lose his mind if she ever up and left on him.

Enjoying the warmth of her brothers' arms, Storm lingered for a few seconds more before Lauryn was climbing over the middle console to give Steven a hug as well.

"Let me grab y'all bags," he said pulling Lau out of the car. Putting her down on the sidewalk, he went to the backseat and got their bags out before moving to the front of the house.

"Ugh... he makes my ass run buttermilk," Amber confessed under her breath once she was beside Stormie. Bursting out laughing, Storm couldn't do anything but shake her head, knowing she was in for a show staying in the house with these two fools.

6

"MY HEART WANTS PEACE WITH MY MIND, I SWEAR ITS TUG OF WAR."

-Sammie

"*I still believe in us... baby don't turn the page. I lay awake at night, tossing and turning, babe.*" Storm sung along with Sammie, singing her heart out while she sat in the tub, soaking. It was 9:30 at night and she had just woken up from a nap only a few minutes ago. Knowing that Amber would wait until the last minute to start getting ready for their night out, Storm decided it was in her best interest to start getting ready now.

After soaking for over thirty minutes, she decided that it was time for her to start cleaning her body. She wasn't sure what time they wanted to leave but she wanted to at least make her and Lau something to eat and get her to bed.

Since getting off of the plane, Lauryn had been on 100, running through the house with Autumn. Storm was just happy that she was happy though. With Luck not being home for the past few weeks, Lauryn hadn't been her normal self. She missed her father's presence at home, as did Storm.

Allowing the water to drain from the tub, Storm started the shower and proceeded to wash her body, lost in her thoughts. Although she was happy to be in New York and with her family, she was wishing that she could be at home with Luck and Lauryn.

Even though she had been miserable while she was home waiting on him to return, at least she was home. She knew that when he did decide to return home, she would be there, but with her here in New York, she would have no idea when he returned home. She also wouldn't be able to talk with him about how they were going to move forward until she returned home herself.

Ten minutes and three washes later, she was stepping out of the shower. With a towel wrapped around her, she stood in the mirror as she prepared to brush her teeth, admiring herself. Like Amber had said earlier, Storm did look horrible. Her skin was inflamed with pimples, her eyes were puffy and there were dark circles around her eyes, indicating that she had been neglecting to get sleep.

'You gotta pull yourself together, Storm... just because you love him doesn't mean that you have to make yourself sick over a conscious decision that he made.' She told herself even though she knew it was easier said than done. However, she was determined to pull herself together. She was only in New York for two weeks and she wanted to enjoy it.

"Finally, I thought you got sucked down the drain." Steven commented as soon as Storm walked out of the bathroom.

"I wasn't even that long."

"You been in there for over an hour."

"Just because your dirty ass hops in the shower and jumps out doesn't mean that we all do. I gotta make sure I'm clean."

"Girl, bye!" He said, pulling a laugh from Storm.

Following her in her room, Steven sat on the bed that Storm and Lauryn would be occupying.

"I hope you ain't wear them clothes outside and you sitting on the bed with them." She fussed at him before he had a chance to get comfortable.

Jumping up from his spot, he held his hands up in surrender. "My bad, I forgot you were anal about shit like that."

"Yeah, now can you get me a new cover and step out so that I can get dressed?"

"I got you, I'll be right back."

As soon as he walked out of the room, Storm was behind him closing and locking the bedroom door so that she could put her shea butter on and throw on some sweats for the moment.

Opening the door, she was shocked to see Steven leaning against the door frame.

"Shit! Why your creepy ass just standing there like that?" Storm asked with a hand over her heart.

Laughing, Steven shook his head and walked into the room. "The devil must be riding you... Ain't no reason you should be scared when I just said that I was coming right back."

"Whatever, nigga. Wassup?" She asked, taking the cover from his hands.

"Have you heard from him?"

"Nope... not a word. He gave Lauryn a cell phone to contact him. A part of me wanted to take his number out of the phone and call him, but I can't bring myself to do it. Husband or not, I'm not chasing him. He left on his own, he'll find his way back when he's ready, on his own."

"I feel you, but that's your husband. Don't let your pride stop you from going and getting your husband back, Storm. You love that man... you know you would be fucked up if this shit became permanent."

"I would, Steven. I won't lie about that at all. However, he has my number. If he wanted to get in contact with me, he knows how to reach me. I live in a house that he purchased for him, myself, and our daughter. He's resided there for the last three and a half years as have I. He knows the address there very well. He's also been paying my cell phone bill for the last five years, he has my e-mail address, my social media handles... he knows how to contact me." Storm said, feeling as if she'd made her point. "I'm not going to jump through hoops to find him. He didn't even have the decency to allow me to explain anything. I didn't even do that surgery, but he would know that if he hadn't run away like a little bitch." Storm could feel herself getting worked up, so she shut up and plopped down on the bed that she had just remade.

"All of that is true, but damn... which one of y'all are going to say enough is enough? Just like I know you've been going through it; I can bet my last dollar that he's been going through it too. But y'all being stubborn as hell right now. Not just you, him too."

"I hear you and I appreciate you saying all of this, but you're saying it to the wrong person. The last time he ran, I told him that was his last time. My feelings, my wishes... none of that is going to get overlooked this time. I'll be damned if he thinks that every single time, we have a dispute, he can run. I'm not setting that example for Lauryn. Regardless of whether he realizes it or not, he's setting an example for her and it's not one I want her to believe is right. So, for that reason I'm not reaching out to him. If he wants to make this right, he can. I'm open to listen, unlike him." Storm told Steven, finalizing that the conversation was over by getting up from her spot on the bed.

Walking over to Storm, Steven wrapped her in his arms and gave her a kiss on the top of her head. "I get it and I respect everything that you just said. I just want to see you happy and I know that Luck is where your happiness lies."

"True. He makes me happy, but my happiness lies in me."

Shaking his head, Steven released her from his embrace, but Storm didn't let him go.

"Speaking of happiness and being that you're giving out all of this advice, let me give you some. I don't know what's up with you and Am but listen to me when I tell you that at some point, she's going to get sick and tired of being sick and tired. When she gets to that point, there will be no getting her back. Don't lose your wife messing around with someone who doesn't even amount to half of her." Steven tried to butt in and speak his peace, but Storm raised her hand and shook her head no telling him that she didn't want to hear it. "You don't have to plead your case to me. You are my brother and regardless, I'm going to always have your back and support you, but I'm telling you as an outsider looking in. Your luck is running short on this. Just think about everything that you have to lose and weigh it against whatever you believe that you can gain from no longer being with Am. Besides losing the one woman besides Mama and I whose always been down for you, think about your daughter and her living in a household separate from you. Not to mention Amber will move on at some point... that love you know she has for you won't stop a thing." Storm finally let him go and bent over to pick up the cover that she had stripped from the bed.

"I love you." She told him as she made her way out of the room, leaving Steven there with his thoughts.

"STORM!" Erin yelled, the second she walked into Am and Stevens house, with Damia right behind her. Heading upstairs to the room that she knew Storm would be occupying, she was filled with excitement.

"Where are you going? I'm down here!" Storm shouted from the table where her, Autumn and Lauryn were sitting and eating their food. The three of them had been sitting in those same spots for the past hour.

It was creeping up on eleven at night and Amber had just gone to start getting herself ready about a half an hour ago. Thankfully, Storm had already showered, done her make-up, with the assistance of the girls, and laid her clothes out for the night.

Now, she was putting some food on her stomach and chatting it up with the minis until it was time for her to get dressed. She had ordered pizza for the house and her and the girls were tearing it up.

Hearing Erin's heels clicking against the floor and Damia trailing behind her, Storm stood up from the table and walked around it to greet Erin and Damia at the entrance to the kitchen.

"Ahhh!" Erin screamed like it had been years since she had seen Storm when in fact it had only been a few months.

"Hi E!" Storm responded to Erin's wails with a smile on her face while the two held onto each other, rocking side to side.

"I've missed you."

"I speak to you just about every day."

"What does that mean?" Erin asked, letting Storm go and giving Lauryn and Autumn the same salutation that she had given Storm.

"Hi, pretty girl." Storm squatted down until she was at Mia's level and gave her a hug and a kiss.

"Hi," Mia shyly responded as she always did when she didn't see Storm for long periods of time.

"You ready to drive Steven crazy with the girls?" Storm asked, tickling her in the process.

With a toothless smile, Mia told Storm that she was ready before Storm let her go be with the girls.

"You aren't dressed yet? I thought if anyone would be ready, it would be you." Erin was following behind Storm upstairs to her bedroom.

"All I have to do is put my clothes on. You should be worried about the snail in the other room."

"I heard that!" Amber said, walking out of the bathroom, towards the ladies in her underwear and bra. She had just finished putting her makeup on. She still needed to touch her hair up a little before she got dressed but it wouldn't take her long.

"She ain't lying." Erin co-signed, giving Am a hug before peeking her head in Steven and Amber's room. "You fully dressed in there, Steve?"

"Why wouldn't he be?" Amber snarled drawing a few head shakes from the girls.

Walking into her room, Storm closed the door behind her while she undressed and prepared to take her clothes off when Erin barged in.

"You know, when the door is closed, that is mostly because the person behind the door doesn't want to be bothered."

"Whatever," Erin retaliated for lack of a better response. Closing the door behind her, she started towards the bed to sit when Storm stopped her.

"Don't you sit on my clean cover with your dirty outside clothes. Either go get a chair or cop a squat in the corner."

"Ugh... you and this pettiness. You still carry on like that all these years later?"

"How is me being clean, petty?"

Rolling her eyes, Erin didn't bother responding. Knowing

Storm, she would have a rebuttal for whatever she had to say, and Erin wasn't in the mood for it.

"What are you wearing tonight?" Erin asked, changing the subject.

"This little number right here." Storm said, lifting her dress from the bad. It was a one armed, sequin, mini black dress that Storm was dying to wear. The sleeve had a tulle ruffle detail that brought the dress out even more. She had found it on Fashion Nova a few weeks ago and couldn't resist it.

"Oh, girl, that shit is fire!"

"Thank you. I've been dying to put this on."

"I hope you know we will be taking pictures and you will be posting on tonight. Luck is about to see all that he been missing."

Rolling her eyes, Storm didn't bother to respond. She had refrained from posting on social media for the past couple of weeks mainly because she wanted Luck to miss her. She figured if he couldn't see her at all, he would return home faster but clearly that didn't work.

Thinking about the conversation she'd had with Steven earlier and the pep talk she'd given herself, Storm decided that Erin was right. It was time that she started back living as she normally did. Tonight, she was going to take a gang of pictures and post the ones she loved. In the back of her mind, all she could think was that maybe, it would give Luck the incentive to contact her.

"IT'S EMPTY IN HERE," Storm commented the second the ladies had made it into the club. The music was blasting, the lights were dimmed, and the ambiance was good, but there were no people. For all of this, Storm could have been at home with the kids painting their nails or something.

"It's still early, Storm. Give it an hour or so." Amber said, prompting Storm to look at her watch.

"Early, bitch it's after midnight... damn near one. If the people ain't here yet, they ain't coming." Storm screamed over the music that was blasting for clearly no apparent reason.

"Here you go with this complaining shit." Amber fussed. She loved Storm like the sister she never had biologically, but she had to admit that Storm was a whiner. If Storm wasn't happy with something, she was going to make sure you knew and everyone around you.

"Yep, and I could have complained from the house and saved my lil' dress." Storm retorted.

"Alright, alright... y'all over here going back and forth, that ain't gonna change shit. The only way to have a good time is to have a good time. What y'all wanna drink?" Erin spoke up, walking to the bar. She never bothered to check and see if Storm and Am were behind her, she was sure that eventually, they would find their way, and she was right.

"If I'm drinking tonight, you already know what I'm drinking."

"I guess being that we took an Uber, we can all have the same. It's turn up time," Amber was back in good spirits with the mention of drinks.

While Erin ordered three Long Island Ice Teas, Storm went and found a section for the three of them. After paying for it, she went back to the bar to direct the ladies to where they would be sitting.

"Thank God for this section because these are not standing or walking shoes. These are look cute while sitting shoes." Erin commented, drawing laughs from Am and Storm.

"Let's toast." Amber said, raising her glass above her head while waiting for the ladies to do the same.

"What are we toasting to?" Storm inquired.

"To Storm being in New York for a few weeks and to all the laughs and good times we are going to have over those two weeks."

"I'll drink to that!" Storm and Erin said, simultaneously.

The three women sat around people watching and making small conversation as the lounge started to fill up. After an hour of people watching, the ladies were ready to make moves. Although the DJ was spinning good music, it wasn't as live in there as the women had expected it to be.

"Yeahhhhh, so..." Storm started but was quickly cut off by Amber.

"Already?" She whined. "We've only been here for an hour."

"It's boring as fuck in here, Am. We don't gotta go home but we sure gotta get the hell up out of here." Storm reiterated with Erin co-signing as she grabbed her clutch from the table in front of her.

"Well, where else are we gonna go? I'm not in a rush to go back home." Amber sucked her teeth as she gathered her purse also.

"It's a million places we can go... it doesn't have to be a lounge or a club, Amber." Erin spoke up trying to diffuse whatever was brewing. She could tell that Amber was feeling a bit outnumbered.

Once the ladies were all together, they made their way to the exit. Just as they approached the door, a group of three men walked in. Even though none of the ladies were checking for a man, they couldn't deny how fine these three men were who stood in front of them.

"Damn," Amber whispered as she continued to eyeball the three men.

"Let's go, y'all" Storm remarked, coming back to her senses.

"You are killing all of the fun tonight." Amber responded as she fell in stride with Storm and Erin again.

"You fine as fuck." One of the men said as he grabbed Amber's left hand to stop her from walking away from him.

"Thank you," Amber looked back at him and smiled while trying not to break her stride. However, the tight hold the handsome stranger had on her wrist, prevented her from moving anymore. "You gonna let me go or what?" Amber asked, flirtatiously.

"After I have your number stored..." he told her, reaching into his back pocket with his other hand to retrieve his cell phone.

"See, had you grabbed my hand and not my wrist, you would have felt the rock my husband put on my hand a few years ago..." Amber replied. Although things were rocky between her and Steven, the fact still remained that they had taken vows in front of God. Despite Steven not holding up his end of the bargain, Amber knew two wrongs didn't make a right.

"Damn..." the guy said after taking a second to check out the ring that was surely adorning Amber's left ring finger. "Are you happy?" He asked, not wanting to accept the fact that she was already spoken for.

"Does it matter?" Amber asked, finally pulling away from the guy and heading out of the door behind E and Storm.

Silence followed the ladies until they were finally in the Uber heading to L'Express for a late-night dinner.

"You good, Am?" Storm inquired, after Amber's silence had driven her crazy.

"Do I have a choice? I got a little girl to think about... I have to be good for her."

"True." Erin said, unsure of what else to say. Silence crept up on them again and this time, they enjoyed it, each lost in their own thoughts until they arrived at the restaurant.

7

"ALWAYS ON MY MIND..."

-Brandy

"*L*au, let's go mama." Storm shouted from the top of the basement stairs before she went back into the living room where Amber was sitting on the couch with the remote in one hand and her cell phone in the other.

"What time are you guys getting back?"

"I'm not sure. I'm just going to go and see Adelasia and my mom then I'm heading back. We'll probably just take them both to get some food and hang for a while before heading back."

"Okay, well I'm gonna go do a head and I guess we will meet up here later."

"You only have one head to do today?"

"Yep, it's a light day and I plan on taking advantage of it."

"Well, what you wanna do?"

"Go shopping."

"Alright, we'll I'm game. Call Erin and let her know. Shoot, how long is it gonna take you to finish that head? We might as well meet at the mall."

"I should be done by three," Amber said after taking a peek at the clock.

"Alright, we'll meet up by 4 then. That gives us more than enough time to run our mouths."

"Yeah right... not with your mom and Luck's mom. They talk, talk." Amber said making Storm burst out laughing with her silliness.

"Don't be talking about my mamas! I fight!"

"MAMA!" Lauryn shouted excitedly the second Adelasia got in the car.

"My babies!" Adelasia responded just as excited. Once she was situated in the car, she leaned over and hugged Storm before reaching back and hugging Lauryn. "Mio figlio?"

Storm didn't verbally respond to her; she just shook her head and took off to go and get her mother.

After picking up her mother and arriving at Sant Ambroeus for brunch, they got comfortable and the questions that Storm really didn't want to answer started flowing.

"So, what are you doing in New York without your husband?"

"Do we have to do this now? With Lau sitting here, soaking everything up like a sponge." Storm cut her eyes at Lauryn, who just as she had suspected, was looking in her mouth as she spoke.

"Here Lauryn, use Mama's phone. Put the headphones in and go to one of those weird videos you kids like to watch of the kids playing with the same toys y'all have." Storm's mother, Pam said causing Storm and Adelasia to laugh.

Once the headphones were secure in Lau's ears and she had

pressed play on the video, the conversation picked back up where it had left off at.

"So, about that son of mine." Adelasia asked, not wasting any time.

Shaking her head, Storm could feel the waterworks ready to start. Having to explain the situation to their parents was embarrassing, to her.

"I don't even know where to start."

"The beginning..."

For an hour, Storm sat there and told the two mothers all about the transgressions going on in her home while they shook their heads and sympathized with the young couple. They had no idea that things were as bad as they were between them. They knew that Storm had miscarried a time or two because their excitement had prompted Storm and Luck to tell them both of the new addition to the family, prematurely. However, they had no idea that they had been struggling like this for the past five years.

"Why didn't you tell us what was going on between you two?"

"It's embarrassing... I don't know what's wrong with me. I'm a woman, I'm supposed to be able to bear children, that's what my purpose is and I can't even do that."

"Cut out that foolish talk," Adelasia scolded Storm before reaching across the table and grabbing Storms hand.

"Well, why does he think that you had the surgery?" Pam asked the million-dollar question that Storm had no clue the answer to.

"I have no idea... I don't even know how he knew about the appointment but somehow he knew."

"And he changed his number?" Adelasia asked. That would explain why she hadn't been able to reach Luck for the past few days. She had been Facetiming and texting him with no response which was nothing like his normal routine. Sure, there were times when she was unable to reach him but never for this long.

"Yep. I haven't talked to him since the morning I was supposed to have the surgery done. He's popped up at Lau's school a time or two but since his last visit with her, he hasn't tried to reach out to her."

"You two need to talk..."

"I know that... I want to talk but he's running. I don't know what else I'm supposed to do."

"Is that the only way you can reach him?" Pam asked, knowingly.

"Yeah." Storm responded not catching on to what her mother was implying.

"So, you can't contact him through that social media stuff y'all do? You can find him on the internet."

"Why should I have to jump through those hoops to speak with him? He's the one running."

"He is, but you are going to have to take accountability for your part in this matter as well... you went behind his back. Even if you didn't agree to not do the surgery, you knew he wasn't on board. You two are married now, important decisions like that should be agreed upon and if an agreement cannot be reached, then you guys have to keep working on it until some kind of compromise is made. Besides, is your pride more important than your marriage? Because that's all I'm hearing." Adelasia butt in to speak her peace.

"I agree, Storm. You have to at least give it a try. There are other ways to reach him other than by phone, baby."

Huffing and puffing, Storm didn't know what to say. Well, she knew what she wanted to say but she would never utter those words to either of the two women sitting in front of her.

"I hear what you both are saying and under different circumstances, I would do whatever you two felt like I needed to do but not this time. He's wrong... I've bent over backwards for him time and time again. Not this time." And Storm meant what she said. Had the circumstances been a little different, she would have been going hard trying to locate Luck and fix her marriage. This time though, Luck needed to fix the mess that was currently their marriage.

"How was lunch with the old people?" Am asked Storm. Storm and Lauryn had arrived at the salon about fifteen minutes ago, but Amber still had someone in her chair. So, Storm had started cleaning up for Amber so there would be less work for her to do when she was finished.

"It was lunch with the old people. The two of them tried to talk me into going back to LA to track Lucky down and work out our differences."

"Well, there is nothing wrong with that... that is your husband, you know."

"Yeah, I know... just like he knows that he's my husband as well."

"Storm..."

"Amber, just leave it alone, please. I don't want to talk about this anymore than I already have."

Throwing her hands up in the air as if she was surrendering, Amber shook her head before saying 'okay'. Thirty minutes later, Storm, Lauryn, Amber and Autumn were in their respective cars and heading to the mall.

"This is just what I need." Storm said once the ladies were all in the mall.

"Some retail therapy, huh?" Amber asked, even though she already knew the answer.

"You know it."

"So, have you started planning the girl's trip, yet?"

"Truthfully, no... I forgot all about that trip."

"Well, what about the BET Awards next weekend in LA? Plus, I saw that Luck was nominated for a few awards."

"Ugh... I should have known." Storm rolled her eyes at Amber as they continued to stroll through the mall.

"Come on, Storm... Erin and I are dying to go to LA and what better time than when the awards are taking place and when Luck is being honored also."

"For starters, we don't even know if Luck is gonna win that award or if we're even gonna see him. Shit, he hadn't been home in two weeks when I was there... and I haven't heard from him since I been here, so God only knows where he is."

"Who cares... this will be our girls' trip. Luck ain't the reason we're going. I just figured it would be dope for us to be there to support his win, should he win."

"Well, it sounds like I've been out voted anyway. If that's what you and Erin want to do, then I guess that's what we're doing."

Even though Storm wanted to throw a fit, in the same breath, she was happy to be going home. Everything in her being was telling her that this time around, her and Luck would be crossing paths and there would be nothing that he could do to prevent it.

8

"LIKE BREEZY SAID, THESE NIGGAS AIN'T LOYAL."

-Keyshia Cole

"So, how are we supposed to do this?" Erin asked as Storm, Amber, and her rode in their Uber to Storm and Luck's house. The ladies had landed about an hour and forty-five minutes ago and were ready to enjoy their time in LA for the weekend. Thanks to the BET Awards, there were plenty of events for the ladies to enjoy. Deciding not to pack much, Erin and Amber only had a carry on alongside of their purses while Storm only had her purse. They planned on going shopping and buying everything that they would need as soon as Storm ran by her house to grab a few things she would need for her stay; her car included.

"Easy, I'll run in really quick and grab what I need and my car keys. Y'all can wait for me outside, it'll only take me a minute." Storm's head was buried in her phone as she scrolled through

Luck's Instagram account. This was how she'd been keeping tabs on him as of late. He hadn't posted much recently but she could still guess what was going on in his life lately by the little that he did post. He was being honored this weekend at an event that the Universal Hip Hop Museum was putting on, participating in the BET Celebrity Basketball Game, and was nominated for an award at the award show, hence the pop-up visit that the girls had pulled. Unbeknownst to Luck, they were going to be supporting every single one of his appearances.

"Orrrrrr, we can all come in the house with you... shit, Erin's never seen the inside of your house and I could use another drink." Picking her head up out of her phone, Storm looked to Amber before rolling her eyes and shaking her head.

"Of course, you would want another drink. You should want a damn nap." Amber had drunk at least five drinks on the plane, she should have been drunk by now. Instead, she was ready to drink some more. This was the first time in a long time... shit, years that she'd been without Autumn. She wasn't complaining because she loved spending time with her talkative baby, but this adult time was much needed.

About an hour later, they were pulling up to Storm and Luck's estate. Thanks to the awards and the usual LA traffic, it had taken them an extra thirty minutes or so to make it there. As the Uber pulled through the gates of the estate and rounded the driveway, Stormie realized that Luck's car was parked in front. Butterflies invaded her stomach temporarily before she realized that there was another car in front of her house. A car that she wasn't familiar with sitting directly in back of Luck's car.

"Whose car is this?" She questioned aloud drawing Erin and Amber's attention to the two cars in front of the house.

"Oh shit..." Erin mumbled as they came to a stop. Looking at the license plate, the three ladies each read it out loud. "Queen K."

Under normal circumstances, Storm would have thanked the cab drive and wished him well, but right now, all she could focus on was the car and the person that it belonged to. Making a quick exit, she jumped out of the car even before the driver could bring the car to a complete stop.

Filing out behind Storm, Erin and Amber rushed to grab their bags from the trunk before running up the stairs, taking them two at a time in order to catch up to Storm. It didn't take long for the ladies to find her. The second they stepped foot inside of the foyer, they heard Storm's voice.

"So, that's your word?"

Looking at each other with wide eyes, the duo took off like lightening to make it to her, dropping their bags in the foyer along the way.

"Oh, hell no!" Amber exclaimed, the second that she was able to see what Storm was seeing.

Luck was sitting on the couch with jeans and sneakers on, but he was without a shirt. Next to him was a light skinned woman either scantily dressed or missing a few items.

Taking the time to take in the woman sitting on her couch, Storm couldn't believe her eyes. This woman had nothing on her... though she was beautiful in her own right. Whoever this woman was, she had a slim build, big lips, and big eyes that were a bit glossed over. Her hair and makeup were a mess, a clear indication of the activities that she'd partaken in prior to the ladies' presence. However, it didn't take anything away from her... yet and still, she was average compared to Storm. Not just in looks, but confidence, demeanor, and all.

Luck's face registered the shock that he was currently in. There was no way Kara would be here had he known that Stormie and the girls would be popping up. He hadn't seen or spoken to Storm in over a month, but here she was.

He had come home two weeks ago, expecting to find Stormie and Lauryn here at their house. To his surprise, they weren't there. Still upset with her and not ready to have the conversation that he knew they would have to have; he didn't even bother reaching out to her. After two weeks of hearing nothing from her, he figured there was nothing more to say. Hence the reason Kara was here today.

Luck had been so angry at Storm that he had allowed that anger to rule his being. But seeing her standing there in the entrance of their living room with the agonizing and resentment filled look on her face, he realized his mistake. His anger dissipated the second he saw her. Gone were the thoughts of divorce, at least on his end. Storm on the other hand was done. This was a new low for them. Never had the two of them gone through anything of this nature. Not only was Luck cheating, he was in the house that she had picked out... the house their daughter called home. *Never shit where you lay your head, nigga!* She wished that he could read her mind at the moment. This was her safe haven... whenever the outside world became too much for her, her home had always given her solace. Not anymore though.

With embarrassment present on her face, Luck's company, Kara, jumped up from the space that she had been occupying and grabbed her belonging.

"Nah, don't bother. You can stay... I'll go." Holding Lucky's stare for a while longer, Storm willed the tears away. She refused to give him or her the satisfaction of seeing how broken she was behind this.

"No, the hell she can't stay—" Erin spoke up before Amber had the chance but was stopped by Storm raising her right hand and shaking her head.

Her voice cracked as she said, "It's not even worth it. Let her have him and all of this..." Looking around the room slowly,

Storm assessed everything she was giving up quickly measuring that it didn't add up to her respect and dignity. "I'm done." With that, she turned on her heels with her head held high and marched out of the house. Amber stood her ground though with Erin at her side. Luck had them fucked up and there was no way they were gonna let this side, even if Storm wanted them to.

"You need to hurry the fuck up." Amber said, attention still on Kara while Lucky jumped up from his seat and ran out of the house after Storm.

Already knowing that the situation wasn't gonna end well, Kara kept her mouth shut and put some pep in her step. Silently, she prayed that she would make it out of the house the same way that she had made it in. Stumbling out of the house with all of her things in hand, she could feel Erin and Amber's presence behind her. As she crossed the threshold of the house, she breathed a sigh of relief, she had made it out. Just as her foot hit the top stair of the porch, she felt a foot in her back before she went tumbling face first down the stairs.

"Amber, No!" Storm shouted, "let's go."

Amber wanted to do more, she had so much pent up anger and frustration that she needed to work off, but she could see that Storm was barely hanging on. Taking heed to Storm's request, Erin and Amber descended the steps and headed to Storm's truck.

Storm stood stoic, hand on her door handle, staring at Luck as he continued to make his way to her. Nothing about him was familiar to her anymore, that revelation alone broke her. Spinning around on the balls of her feet, she grabbed for the car door to grant her access to her seat.

"Storm," Luck finally spoke up as he pushed her door closed from behind her.

Ignoring him, Storm pulled on the door handle once again but was met with resistance. Growing frustrated, Storm turned around to face Lucky, "move, Luciano!"

"Just hear me out, please." He pleaded. He had invaded her space, forcing her to back up into the door. With her back flat against the door, her arms propelled, pushing into Lucky in an attempt to get him away from her.

"I don't want to hear shit. You should have wanted to talk weeks ago... a fucking month ago even. Fuck you!" Storm tried once again to move Lucky away from her so that she could get in the car.

Unmoving, Luck stared at her, begging for her to listen to him, with his eyes. Storm grew infuriated with Luck and that frustration poured out of her with the first punch she threw at him. Connecting with his jaw, Luck's arm immediately went to his face to block her next hit. Amber and Erin could be heard from the car with their "ooh's and oh shit's".

Storm didn't even slow down as she continued to swing until finally, she got tired. There were tears, snot, and hair decorating her face as her breathing struggled to return to its natural state. Taking advantage of Storm's fatigue, Lucky grabbed her in a bear hug, giving her the boost of energy that she desperately needed.

"Get the fuck off of me!" She belted, kicking him and throwing her head back hoping to connect with his mouth or at least his head.

Putting her down momentarily to readjust her in his arms, Luck then quickly grabbed her back up again in a tighter hold. Him walking to the house with Storm caused Amber to open her door and step out of the car.

"Where are you going with her?"

"She's not going with y'all... y'all go ahead and leave her."

"No!" Storm didn't want to be nowhere near him. "I'm not going anywhere with you." She started going crazy in his arms, even more so than she was previously, giving Luck a harder time. He was struggling to carry her but was determined to get her in the house.

"Luck, put her down," Amber was stuck, still standing there with the door in her hand as she contemplated whether she should make her way towards Luck and Storm or not. Had this been anyone else on the street, Amber would have come out of the car swinging, but she didn't involve herself with marital issues. She knew the game, Storm might hate him now, but in a few days or weeks, she'd be loving on him again.

"Amber, mind your business, man." Luck warned her, not breaking his stride.

"She is my business... put her down!" She yelled, inching her way towards Luck as he carried Storm away.

Luck didn't bother responding to her request. There was nothing she could say that would change his mind, this was his wife and they needed to have a conversation. Luck wasn't putting Storm down until she was in the house where he could talk to her without the outside disturbances.

"Storm, tell them to leave. We need to talk, after we talk, you can meet up with them." Luck gritted.

"Fuck you! The only thing you need to do is sign the divorce papers I'll have drawn up tomorrow and then leave me the hell alone."

"That's not an option and you know that..." Finally approaching the house with Amber hot on their tails, he picked up his speed a bit more. Making it in with seconds to spare, he quickly slammed the door and placed his back against it before finally releasing Storm.

Once she had been placed on her feet, she spun around so that she was facing Luck. Continuing her assault; punching, kicking, and screaming for him to move out of her way so that she could get back out of the house. Snot and tears clashed on her face, showing all of her pain, as she tried desperately to get him out of her way. To no avail, Luck refused to move. Succumbing to her emotions, her hits got weaker as her cries got stronger. Not sure what else to do, Luck stood by as Storm had a break down.

Falling to her knees, Storm was having a hard time controlling her breathing. Her heaves and hiccups took over her being as she positioned herself with her back against the wall. Pulling her legs up to her chest, she placed her head between her knees and wrapped her arms around her legs, rocking back and forth in an effort to get her breathing regulated.

Minutes passed before she felt calm enough to lift her head from her knees. Luck stood in the same position, watching on as Storm pulled herself together. Her chocolate brown skin now had a red undertone to it, her eyes were bloodshot red and puffy, and her hair was all over her head.

"I'm sorry," was all Luck could muster up in that moment. After the words left his mouth though, he was kicking himself.

"Fuck your sorry." She muttered, avoiding eye contact with him.

"I know it doesn't change anything—"

"Then keep it to yourself… what is sorry supposed to do for me? For Lauryn? You ruined her chance at a family and this place she called home."

"Don't flip this shit on me. Yeah, I fucked her, but that's because you had already fucked us up!" Luck exclaimed; his face contorted showing the pain that he housed as well. "You went against what the fuck we discussed and went and got that bullshit ass surgery done!"

"I didn't get the fucking surgery!" Storm screamed at the top of her lungs, stunning Luck to silence.

Internally, Luck questioned the words that had just left

Stormie's mouth. *She didn't get the surgery.* He recalled everything from the day that he had gotten the notification for the surgery on his phone before looking for and finding the paperwork. He even recalled the day that she left the house to get the surgery done. The second she left the house on the day of the supposed surgery; he was up and packing him a bag. He never even waited it out to see what would happen once Storm returned home.

"Yeah, you're standing there looking stupid now, huh? I never got the surgery. I wanted my marriage... I wanted my family, and I still don't have either one." Her voice cracked as she came to that revelation.

"I thought—"

"Had you not run, you would have known that, Luciano." All of the fight had left Storm.

"I'm so sorry, Stormie."

Not sure what to say or how to respond, Storm shook her head. She was over this conversation already. There should have been no reason for an apology, yet there he was standing against the door still with his hands in his pocket and his head hung low, apologizing to her.

"Tell me something I don't know." Getting up from her spot on the floor, Storm got up and headed to the room Luck and her used to share. There was some stuff that she needed to pack for herself and for Lauryn as they wouldn't be returning there.

Figuring that she was going to get comfortable, Luck headed to the living room. Pulling his cell phone out of his pocket before he got comfortable, he decided to order some food for the two of them. Being that it had been just him in the house for the past couple of weeks, there was no food there. Trying to do everything to get on Storm's good side, he ordered her all of her favorite dishes from Oliva Trattoria and a few bottles of wine.

Forty minutes later, he had showered, changed his clothes and the food had arrived but Storm was still nowhere in sight. Luck took his time setting up the dining room table and then went on a search for Storm. Going straight to the master bedroom, he was surprised to see that she wasn't there but there was a suitcase sitting by the dresser. Immediately turning around, he made a dash for Lauryn's room where he found Storm putting the last pieces in Lauryn's luggage.

"What are you doing?"

"What does it look like I'm doing?" Storm wasn't in the mood for Luck and his stupid ass questions.

"I should have said, why are you packing Lauryn and your stuff up?"

"Because we no longer live here." Standing up after she zipped the luggage, she struggled to pull it along the carpeted floor to the door.

"The fuck you mean y'all no longer live here? The fuck you think y'all live at?"

"Exactly what I said... you are free to do as you please in this bitch with whoever the fuck you wanna do it with. My child and I won't hold you up."

"You sound stupid." Taking the bag from Storm's hand, he quickly unzipped it and dumped the contents out on the floor.

"You're gonna pack that shit the fuck back up." Storm told him matter of factly.

"Yeah, iight." He laughed at her, making his way out of Lauryn's room door.

Grabbing at his shirt, she prevented him from moving any further than he anticipated.

"Pick this shit the fuck up, Luciano."

"I ain't picking shit up."

"Yes, the fuck you are! Pick my baby's shit up!"

"Storm, you're not taking my daughter anywhere, just like you aren't moving anywhere either."

Deciding not to argue with him anymore, she simply shook her head and turned to the door. Little did he know, Storm would buy back everything she was leaving behind. Luck could win this fight, but ultimately, she was going to win the war. She was going to find a place and have everything replaced in no time.

Seeing that things were not going the way he wanted them to go, he decided to take another approach. Catching up to Storm at the top of the staircase, Luck grabbed her arm, causing her to spin around.

"Can we please just talk about this? I bought some food... we can sit and talk over dinner then if you still aren't in agreement you can leave." Even though Luck knew he wasn't letting her leave if he had a choice.

"There is nothing to talk about, Luciano. I'm good."

"There is a lot to talk about. Regardless of what we have going on, we have a daughter. She deserves for the two of us to be on one accord."

"Here's one accord for you... Lauryn will live with me and you can have her on holidays and extended breaks from school."

"Get the fuck out of here, Storm. You must have smoked some good shit before you came here with all this stupid shit spewing out of your mouth." Luck said, all but foaming at the mouth.

"I guess you'll see." Turning back around, Storm started down the stairs before the desperation in Luck's voice stopped her.

"Please Storm... can we just talk about this over dinner, please?"

Even though she hated him at this moment, the sound of him hurting, even if it was nothing compared to her hurt, did something to her. She wanted to say no, she wanted to act on her hurt, say a bunch of shit that she knew would break him, but instead she agreed. Immediately, Luck's mood lightened up as he hurried down the stairs, leading Storm to the table before she had a chance to change her mind.

"WHAT WERE YOU THINKING?" After three big glasses of wine and an hour of staring at Luck from across the table with eyes full of disgust, Storm finally asked the question she had been thinking about all night.

"I was thinking that we were over. I thought you went and got that surgery done and I was so angry. Then I came home weeks ago and you weren't here, and neither was Lauryn... You never came back, never called the house phone. I thought we were done."

"How did you even know I was scheduled to get the surgery that day?"

"It was saved under our joint calendar."

"Wow..."

"Yeah, I couldn't believe you were that slow either."

Storm wanted to have a smart remark to his statement but the truth was that it had been a slow moment on her behalf. For the past few weeks, she had racked her brain on how Luck could have found out when she hadn't told a soul... now she knew.

Conversation seized between the two of them as Storm finished off the rest of her drink. Reaching across the table to get the second bottle of wine that Luck had opened and had sitting on ice, Luck tried to stop her.

"Storm, you don't need no more of that shit," Luck told her, trying to grab the bottle from her. Just as he got ahold of the bottle, she snatched it away, causing it to slip from both of their grips and fall to the table.

Spilling all over the table and Storm, she jumped up to get out of the way just a little bit too late. "Shit, Luck! Look at what you did!" Storm exclaimed as she picked up the bottle from where it was rolling on the table. Standing the bottle upright, Storm stood stoic, trying to get her emotions under wrap. The bottle of wine that she had consumed already was causing her to be an emotional wreck. She could feel tears welling up even though she didn't want to cry, hell, she couldn't even figure out what she would be crying about.

"I'm sorry, let me get something to clean all of this up with." Luck said as he looked at Storm. Her clothes, the table, the chair, and the carpet were all decorated a deep red, courtesy of the wine.

Storm stayed stationed in the same spot that she was standing in, unsure of what to do. Her white pants were ruined as were her white and blush pumps. Shaking her head and saying to hell with it, she stripped out of her pants and shoes.

"Damn," Lucky said as he walked back into the dining area from the kitchen.

Just that quickly, Storm had forgotten that Luck was in the house with her. Placing her hands in front of her to shield herself from his looking eyes, she backed out of the dining room and took the stairs two at a time until she had made it to the room that she used to share with Luck. Walking to the closet, she rummaged through the stuff that hadn't made the cut into her luggage until she found a pair of distressed sweats that she had gotten from Fashion Nova a few months ago.

Making her way to her dresser, she grabbed a camisole and underwear before strutting to the bathroom. As soon as she saw the toilet, the urge to pee took over her being. Throwing her clothes on the bathroom counter, she quickly made her way to the toilet, barely making it to the toilet.

"Ohh," She moaned as she emptied her bladder. Thanks to the

wine in her system, it took her what felt like ten minutes to empty her bladder, or so it felt. Flushing the toilet, she got up and stripped out of the rest of her clothes and then cut the shower on and stepped inside.

Downstairs, Luck rushed around the dining room trying to get everything cleaned up. The second he heard the shower come on, he gave up cleaning completely. Finding his way upstairs, Luck stripped out of his clothes in the hallway before tiptoeing into his bedroom. Peeking through the door, he checked to make sure that Storm wasn't in the room. Hearing her singing lightly, he knew that she was already in the bathroom, in the shower.

He knew that she would give him a hard time about this, but he felt confident in the fact that the wine would sway her judgement, so he made his move. Watching her from the door, his dick grew. Storm was beautiful. Her milk chocolate skin glistened due to the water running off of her. At 150 lbs., she was the perfect size. Unlike all of the women Luck saw on a daily basis in Los Angeles, Storm was completely natural. Her thighs and ass were well proportioned with tiger stripes running all along her ass cheeks. The pudge at her stomach was evident that she had unselfishly given life to their daughter.

Her kinky 4c hair sat on top of her head in a pineapple while her baby hairs and edges danced around her face and neck. Soap suds moved down her back and legs as she twirled under the shower head to rinse herself off. Eyes closed and head slightly elevated to prevent her entire head from getting wet, she didn't see Luck standing in the doorway watching her.

With his hand on his member, he massaged it slowly as he made his way to the shower to join Storm. Sliding the glass door back, he stepped in just as Storm spun around.

"No, Luck... what are you doing? Get out." She demanded

before looking down at his dick in his hands. Even though she was turned on, she was still trying to stand her ground.

"Luck, you need to get out of here." Instead of responding to her, he continued massaging his dick. Watching Storm's nipples harden, he knew that she was aroused, just like he was. Reaching out to grab her nipple between his thumb and pointer, he fell short when Storm stepped out of his reach.

"Lucky, get out..." Storm said more forcefully, even though she really didn't want him to leave. Thankfully for her, her request fell on deaf ears.

"I miss you, Storm." Luck told her, stepping closer to her, closing the space between the two of them. Releasing his dick, he wrapped his arms around her, pressing his dick into her stomach. Using his free hand, he lifted her chin so that she was looking at him.

"I fucked up a lot over the past few months, let me right my wrongs, Storm." Not wanting a response from her at that moment, he kissed her.

When Storm didn't stop him or protest, he proceeded by kissing her again, this time, using his tongue to pry her lips open and dropping his hand to massage and grope her ass.

Wanting to pleasure Storm first, Luck abandoned her lips before squatting down until he was staring at her freshly shaved box. Lifting her right leg, he placed it over his shoulder before placing one hand on the floor of their shower.

With water splashing down on him, Luck disregarded it as he stuck his tongue out. He teased her by licking her bulb repeatedly like a dog drinking from his water bowl. Making his tongue stiff, he proceeded to lick her most sensitive spot applying pressure this time around, which granted him a moan from Storm.

Growing tired of the cat and mouse game that Luck was playing with her, she moved her left hand and placed it on the top of his head. Pulling him closer, she prevented him from pulling away from her. Getting the hint, Luck wrapped his lips around her clitoris and gently sucked. Looking up at Storm, he watched as she threw her head back and opened her mouth before her hips took on a mind of their own and started winding against his mouth.

"Uhh," Storm grunted, further pushing Luck's head into her. Trying not to break the connection between his mouth and Storm's clit, he used his free hand to invade her vaginal hole. Taking a finger at first, he inserted it into her and curled it while he massaged her insides. Feeling her cream and witnessing the way she was bucking her hips, he inserted another finger. Seconds later, Storm was pushing his head away as she tried to run from the pleasure that he was bringing her.

Refusing to let up, Luck ignored her cries to stop as he continued to suck on her clitoris like a newborn baby would their mother's nipple. Not even a full minute later, he felt Storm raining down on his fingers once again.

Feeling like she had had enough, he released her clit and got up from his place on the shower floor. Not wasting time, he hoisted Storm up. Wrapping her legs around Luck's waist, she grabbed his dick and inserted it inside of her.

The intrusion though welcomed was slightly painful. Scrunching her face up momentarily, she rolled her hips aiding the pain in quickly wearing off.

"You feel so good." Luck confessed.

Ignoring him, Storm continued with the task at hand. She could feel her next orgasm building as she moved to the tune of the beat in her head.

"This mine?" Luck questioned. Though he would never say it, he was feeling slightly insecure with how quiet Storm was. Under normal circumstances, he couldn't get Storm to shut the fuck up when they were having sex. Now though, she was mute telling Luck that she was emotionally detached from him and what they were doing at the moment.

Remaining mute, Storm closed her eyes to block out the sight of Luck's face. Yeah, she was allowing him into her cave, but it was for her own benefit. She was horny as fuck and she couldn't picture herself stepping out on her marriage to add another person to her rolodex. So, she would use Luck to get what she needed for the moment, selfishly, if it meant her coming out on top.

Trying to get something out of Storm, Luck put his back into it as he began drilling into Storm without remorse.

Whimpering, Storm stubbornly held on to her silence, not even giving Luck the benefit of hearing her moan.

"Is it mine, Stormie?" Luck asked, going for broke in her pussy.

Unable to maintain her silence any longer, Storm belted out, "Shit!"

Feeling encouraged, Luck continued his assault on her, grabbing one of her nipples in his mouth and biting it. "Ahh," Storm screamed, unwrapping her legs from around Lucky's waist. Pushing her hand between the two of them, she tried to run from the serious dick down he was giving her.

"Nu huh..." Luck spoke, picking Storm's legs back up and wrapping them around his midsection once again. "Stay your ass right here."

Within minutes, Luck was climaxing inside of Storm, with her following right behind him. Wanting to make sure that he buried his seeds as deep inside of her as he could, he continued pumping inside of her well after he was done releasing.

Finally letting her down, he smirked when he saw that her legs were too weak to hold her. Silently applauding himself, he held onto her until he was sure that she had recovered enough to get herself together.

After the two of them were cleaned, they made their way to the bedroom where they carried on with their shenanigans for a few more hours.

9

"YOU CAN PLAN A PRETTY PICNIC, BUT YOU CAN'T PREDICT THE WEATHER."

-Outkast

Tipping into the AIRBNB that her and the girls had rented for the weekend, Storm was not looking forward to the questions she knew they were about to bombard her with. Thankful that they had been thoughtful enough to leave the door open for her, she breathed a sigh of relief as she moved through the darkened house.

Storm had snuck out of her and Luck's home about an hour ago, right after Luck had fallen asleep. For two hours straight, the two of them had gone at it like rabbits. In the moment, it felt good... it felt like home, like everything was right once again between the two of them. When they were finished though, Storm was regretting it, immediately.

Not even 24 hours ago, she had walked in on Luck and another woman doing God knows what, yet she had given herself to him so freely. She was pissed with herself and could only think that had she been Lauryn doing what she'd done, she would be disappointed in her.

Making her way through the living room, Storm gave God a million and one silent thanks that the girls were asleep and not waiting up for her like she had originally thought they would be. Feeling like she was in the clear, she put a lil' pep in her step to make it to the room that would be hers.

'Third room on the left,' Storm recited to herself as she turned the doorknob to the room that she would be occupying for the next week.

Running her hand along the wall until she found the light switch, she flicked the light on and then stepped into the room.

"Look who's just sneaking in at some 3 a.m." Erin joked, scaring Storm. Amber and Erin were seated at the foot of Storm's bed patiently waiting for her.

"Shit..." Storm snarled, "y'all heifers scared the shit out of me. Why the hell are y'all sitting in the dark anyway?!"

Placing her pocketbook and overnight bag that she had packed on the chair that was in the corner of the room, she took off her sweater and moved to rummage through her overnight bag for some pajamas to sleep in

"Uh huh... forget all of that. This doesn't look like what Storm was wearing when we left her at the house, does it, Erin?" Amber inquired, with wide eyes stuck on Storm.

"Mind your business, hoe." Stormie told Amber while pulling some pajama pants out of her bag. Untying the sweatpants that she was wearing, Storm slid them down her legs before stepping out of them and into the pajamas.

"Now it's 'mind your business' but a few days ago, she wanted to tell us all of her business."

"Uh huh, cuz' she wanted us to give her ass some hope and

shit. Now that she got some dick, she walking around feeling like she could handle the world without us." Erin said, causing all three of the girls to laugh at her.

Plopping down on the bed between Erin and Amber, Storm laid back and stared at the ceiling before deciding to come clean about her night with Lucky.

"We had sex..."

"We already knew that... it's written all over your face."

"So, does this mean that the two of you are working things out?" Erin asked, hopeful. She was a sucker for love. Erin had only been in one relationship her entire adult life... which just so happened to be with Damia's father, Dame. Regardless of what went on between the two of them, they were determined to make their relationship work. Even at 17 and 18 years old, they loved each other just that much.

Shaking her head, no, Storm exhaled deeply as she debated on whether to let the ladies in on her most inner thoughts. After a few seconds passed, she finally spoke up. "I feel so stupid for having sex with him... we just walked in the house not even a whole damn day ago and seen him with another woman, he admitted sleeping with her, but yet there I was busting it open for him. I don't know whether him and that woman used condoms... I don't know if she's clean or if she is the only woman he's slept with and yet, there I was being a thot."

"What does that matter Storm? That's your husband. Shit, I would be a thot for my husband too."

"Yeah, I know that he's my husband... but he knew that too. However, he was still in there scantily dressed with her after doing things that were supposed to be only reserved for me."

"I understand where you're coming from, Storm, but you guys have been apart from each other for a month. What did you expect?"

"I expected the same loyalty I give to him in return, Erin. What? Is the fact that it's been a month since we were in each other's presence supposed to give him a pass? Do you think he would be as understanding if he walked in on me?"

"Hell no," Amber exclaimed. "That nigga would have tried to break your neck and the nigga you were with."

"My point exactly. Not to mention he would have been crying about shit not being the same and him no longer being able to trust me. And I could have respected that, the same way he's gonna have to respect this shit being on the other foot. As far as I'm concerned, he's supposed to be the same regardless of whether I'm in his face or not. Shit, I don't care if it would have taken a year before he and I had a conversation, he could have bet his life on the fact that I would have still been holding it down for him."

"A year though, Storm?" Erin asked, doubting that her cousin would have been able to hold it down that long without talking to or sleeping with another man.

"A year is nothing when you really love someone and want to be with them. I could have gone a lifetime if it would have taken us that long to get right. Shit, when I was in college, I went a whole year and a half, almost two years."

"Well, do you think you could ever move past it?" Erin asked, praying that Storm said yes. She loved the relationship Luck and Storm had. Even though she didn't see herself getting involved with anyone else for a while, when she did finally find the one, she wanted their union to be as genuine as Luck and Storm's. They had their shit with them, as did all couples, but the love overrode everything else.

"I don't know, E. I wanna say yes, but right now, I don't see it happening. I'm just so hurt right now... if he just needed time to gather his thoughts, I could have understood that. Even if he needed more space and time, I would have been okay with that too. But to step out on our marriage... I don't know if I can forgive that or if I even want to."

The pangs in her heart made it real for Storm as tears clouded her vision. She was determined not to cry though. She had done enough of that over the month that Luck had isolated himself from her.

"You guys will be okay and the trust you feel is lacking at this moment, will be replenished. I have faith in the two of you if I don't have faith in anything else." Amber said, leaning over to hug Storm. She could feel the sadness and hurt pouring off of Storm and it broke her heart to see her in this state. There wasn't much that brought Storm to this place of grief, but Lucky had the ability to do just that.

"I hope so, but I won't hold my breath." Storm muttered.

"LET'S GO THERE TO EAT." Amber pointed to a restaurant that was in front of them as they drove down Melrose avenue.

"You know this bitch doesn't eat shit." Storm complained, pointing at Erin.

"I'm glad y'all know." Erin smiled with her head still in her phone already knowing that she was the topic of discussion.

"But they have healthy food in there."

"What do you deem as healthy?"

"Salads and shit."

Shaking her head, Erin couldn't do anything but laugh at Amber's ignorance.

"I eat more than some damn salads, bitch. Thank you very much. But if y'all wanna eat this bullshit, go ahead. I'm good, I ate already."

Pulling up to the front of the restaurant where valet was, the ladies all climbed out of the Jeep they were renting for the duration of their stay. Walking into the restaurant, they were seated within five minutes and had placed their orders ten minutes later. As soon as the waiter completed taking their orders and had walked away, their conversation began.

"Have you heard from Steven?" Erin was dying to know. Steven had been blowing up Stormie and Erin's phones recently about Amber and it was driving them both sick.

"Yeah, his ass been calling me. The minute the conversation strays from Autumn, I hang up on his ass. I'm not entertaining his shit anymore. I'm over it."

"I know that's right, sis." Storm agreed with Am before the two of them reached over the table and slapped hands.

"So, you aren't going to let him explain? Or try to fix things at least?" Erin desperately wanted to know. She had been talking Steven off of the ledge for the past couple of weeks and if their relationship wasn't going to work out, then he needed to know.

"Explain what, Erin? He cheated, what more can he say to me?"

"You don't know for sure that he cheated." Erin defended him.

"Erin, if your nigga come home after one in the morning and the first thing he did was make his way to the bathroom to wash his dick, what would you think?" Storm asked her.

"I would think that nigga has some explaining to do."

"He been explaining since we were teenagers. Ain't shit else to explain. We have a daughter. Like Storm said, I don't ever want her to think that because of my actions, love is settling or tolerating disrespect or disloyalty. I never want her to reward pain and dishonesty with love and dedication. You don't stick around waiting for a man to come to his senses, praying that when he finally does come to them, it'll be you he decides to be with. At least, I don't want that shit for Autumn. I've done that shit since I was a teenager, all it's done is set the standard for how Steven treats me now. I'm not showing that shit to my daughter."

Damn... Both Storm and Erin felt her on that.

"That's deep."

None of the ladies had anything more to say when the waiter returned to the table with their food and Erin's slices of avocado.

"Do y'all think all men cheat?" Storm asked, digging into her food. The episode that she walked in on with Luck was stuck in her mind. As much as she tried forgetting about it or pushing it to the back of her mind, it was staying put. She couldn't even close her eyes at night without seeing Luck and that woman sitting on her couch with parts of their clothing on.

"Nah, I don't believe that all men cheat. I do however think that they'll try that shit once though and it'll be up to you to show them that you ain't with that shit. That's where I fucked up at. I kept on fighting, trying to show Steven that I was it for him, not even realizing that I was showing him that I was okay with the shit he was doing to me."

It was like the sky opened up for rain showers on a sunny day the way that Amber went from talking calmly to crying hysterically. The pain of her reality struck her like lightening.

Erin and Storm were so used to seeing Am keep it together and be the strong one out of the group, that they were both momentarily paralyzed with shock and confusion. Regrouping quickly, the two moved their seats closer to where she was sitting and did their best to comfort her.

"I'm okay," Amber said, putting her hands up to prevent the ladies from coddling her and making this emotional moment worse. She knew that the minute she was wrapped in one of their arms, there would be no way of stopping the tears that she had used to water her anger and frustrations.

Once she had contained herself, she continued talking. "This shit just hurts... coming to the realization that I allowed this. God kept giving me signs and I just kept on ignoring it. I could have put myself out of this misery a long time ago. I just kept holding on, swearing I knew what was best for me... better than God." Chucking, Amber shook her head. "Could you believe that? I thought I knew better than God."

Just that quickly, Amber had lost her appetite and Storm was right behind her. Although Amber had no intention of turning Storm off from Luck, that's exactly what she was doing. All she could think of was the fact that if she allowed him back in her life, she would be telling him she was okay with what he had done or hadn't done for that matter. She didn't want to get into the habit of accepting anything that she knew in the long run would be detrimental to her happiness and security.

"I'm sorry y'all. I know this wasn't what today or this trip was for."

"You don't have anything to apologize for, Amber. This trip is exactly for this. We needed mental health days and who else but us to give each other the counseling we need?" Storm said, scooting her chair back to her place at the table.

"Have you heard from Lucky yet today?" Amber asked, thankful to change the conversation.

"He called me a few times, but I really don't have anything to say."

"Well, let him do the talking, sis."

"Not if it's gonna result in me on my back."

"Then meet him somewhere else. Shit, go to the beach tonight or something." Erin spoke up.

"I didn't come here for that... I mean, sure, I planned on seeing my husband and maybe fixing what was damaged in our relationship, but the damage is even worse than I thought. I'm not equipped for this repair... I brought the wrong tools."

"You can't run forever, Stormie. You talked about him running, you're doing the same. At some point, you're gonna have to put on your big girl panties and deal with this shit like a woman." Amber told Storm.

"Yeah, I know. It just won't be today."

Forty-five minutes later, the ladies were pulling up to the flea market at the Melrose Trading Post. Storm loved this place, every Sunday Storm and Lauryn found themselves down there walking around for hours buying things that they really had no need for.

"Damn, look at all of these people." Amber said as she looked around the lot that had been transformed into a huge flea market.

"Forget about all of these people, we're going to be charcoal by the time we leave out of here. Storm, why you bring us here?" Erin complained.

"Because you are going to love it." Storm replied covering her face with her sunglasses and grabbing the ticket from the parking aid.

Strolling through the market, the ladies talked, laughed, and bought a little of everything. Two and a half hours later, the ladies were finally leaving the flea market and heading back to the AirBNB.

"What are we doing later?" Erin asked feeling beat from being out in that Los Angeles sun all day. She was moving to her bedroom with her bags in tow not even waiting for a response from Storm.

"Later? We're only here to change and then we were heading to Santa Monica beach." Storm said looking at Erin like she was crazy. Who came on a vacation to sleep?

"The beach? I thought we were going somewhere tonight..."

"We are... there's a party tonight that we'll be attending."

"Who's party and where at?" Amber asked, praying it was someone or something good. She was all for the running around.

It had been a lifetime since she had been able to run free without Autumn following her every move... or at least, that's how it felt.

"Puff is having a house party..."

"Puff Daddy?!" Erin and Amber screamed at the same time.

"Yes, and please get all of that screaming and shit out now. Don't go to this man's house and embarrass me tonight, please." Storm begged, grabbing her swimsuit out of her bag.

"Yeah, I'm definitely not going to the beach, now... I need to be well rested. If what the blogs and shit say about Puff's house parties, I need to be on point... that means no bags under my eyes, no sand lost in my hair and shit." Erin said, causing Storm to roll her eyes.

"You have bags under your eyes on the regular." Storm taunted. "It won't be nothing new."

"Fuck you, Storm!" Erin stuck her middle finger up for the added effect as she walked away to her room to prepare for her shower and nap, leaving Amber and Storm standing in Storm's room.

"So, do you think Luck will be there tonight?"

"I'm sure he will..." Storm responded, trying to sound unbothered. The truth was though, she had thought about that all day. She was unsure whether he would be bringing anyone with him or not and she was worried about it. It was one thing for Luck to be entertaining people in private, especially with him being a public figure. However, she would more than lose it if he brought his *friend* with him to an event where their circle would be present.

"You don't plan on talking to him before the party? It's gonna be awkward... don't you think?"

Shaking her head, Storm stayed quiet. She knew it was gonna be awkward and for the sake of saving face, she knew she would have to carry on with Luck like everything was good in their lives when the reality was that it wasn't.

"Come on, Storm... you have to talk to him."

"I'll talk to him when I get there, Am... not that there is really anything more to say. He said everything yesterday."

"Clearly there is more to say if you and him aren't on good terms yet. Shit, if he said that much yesterday, you should be at home riding his dick instead of cooped up with Erin and I for a girl's trip. You haven't been with your husband before yesterday in over a month."

"Yeah, he said a mouth full yesterday, but it wasn't anything to change the fact that things between us will never be the same. He cheated and if he didn't, he should have because regardless of what he says, that's how I feel."

"I understand, but Storm..."

"No, don't Storm me... if you had walked into your house and seen Steven with another woman sitting on your couch the way I seen Luck, there would be nothing I could say or God himself could say to you to change your mind about what you were feeling." Standing up from her spot on the floor, Storm grabbed her towel and toiletries before heading to the bathroom. "I'm going to get in the shower, I'll see you when it's time to go... we're only going to the beach, Am so please don't take all day getting ready. I'm trying to be out of here in the next forty-five minutes."

"Forty-five minutes?!" Amber exclaimed. "That's not even enough time for me to shower."

"Listen man... I will leave your ass. You ain't doing shit but going to the beach and you're going to shower when you make it back in the house before we party tonight. Just do a bird bath or some shit."

"See, I always knew your ass was dirty giving me suggestions like that." Amber said, getting up and leaving out of Storm's room before she could respond.

THIRTY MINUTES LATER, Storm and Amber were in the car heading to Venice Beach.

"I gotta make a stop first."

"Do what you gotta do." Amber told her, further reclining her seat and turning up the music.

A little while later, they were pulling up to a rundown store front in what appeared to be the hood to Amber.

"Where the hell are we at, Storm?" Amber asked, sitting up and hitting the lock button on the doors. The people she was seeing looked a bit sketchy to her and she wanted no parts.

"This is one of my favorite dispensaries. The have some of the best edibles I've ever tasted." Storm answered her while turning around to grab her pocketbook out of the backseat. "You want something out of here?"

Amber had never had an edible before, so she had no idea what she wanted. "Get me whatever you're getting."

"Okay," climbing out of the car, Storm didn't even make it to the sidewalk before she heard the doors lock once again. She turned to look at Am through the window and laughed before she continued inside of the dispensary, ready to spend a pretty penny.

Almost 20 minutes later, Storm was emerging from the store with a bag full of goodies.

"What the hell you get all of that shit for?" Amber exclaimed before Storm could fully get back in the car.

"We're here for a week, why wouldn't I get all of this?"

"You have a problem." Amber replied, shaking her head at Storm.

"Don't judge me, heifer... we're here for a few days."

Arriving at the beach, the ladies grabbed their belongings out of the trunk and went to find a good spot on the beach.

"UMM, THIS SHIT IS GOOD!" Amber exclaimed taking another piece of the THC infused lemon bar that Storm had passed her way.

"Your ass better slow down... that shit gonna hit you hard and you won't be no good tonight." Storm warned.

"I got this, Storm... I don't even feel anything."

"That's how it starts... next thing you know, you'll be slumped."

Ignoring Storm, Amber continued snacking away while Storm sunbathed, and people watched until her phone distracted her.

"Who is that?" Amber inquired after watching Storm ignore the phone call that came in the first time before the phone started ringing again.

"Luck with his annoying behind."

"Why he gotta be all that?"

"Cuz he is... this nigga done called me over thirty times since I left the house."

"And you ain't answer not one call?" Amber questioned, surprised at Stormie's will. For as long as she could remember, there was never a time when Storm could resist Luck. Even back in the days, she would say she wasn't fucking with him but then they'd be talking and the best of friends after a few days.

"I really don't have anything to say... I'm still stuck on what I walked in on yesterday."

"You can't be that stuck, sis... you were in bed with him not even two hours later."

"Fuck you! I was tipsy as fuck and had a lapse in judgement." Storm laughed, starting to feel the effects of the brownie she had eaten.

"I'm just saying..." Amber responded taking another piece of her lemon bar.

Silence consumed the two women as they sunbathed, and people watched for a few more minutes before something caught Amber's eyes at the towel next to them.

"Look at that!" Amber exclaimed, shooting up from where she had been laying.

"What?" Storm asked, turning her head in the direction that Amber was looking in. Storm wasn't sure whether or not she needed to fight or flee but she was gonna be on point, regardless.

"You see those seagulls over there? Look at how they are attacking those people's stuff!" Amber said before laughing her behind off.

Looking at the blanket that the seagulls were attacking, Storm had to laugh also. Whoever had been sitting there had left bags of chips on their blanket and inside of their opened bags and the seagulls had gotten ahold of it before turning the chips up on the blanket and devouring it. However, the way Amber was laughing at the scene in front of them made Storm laugh even harder.

"You're fucking high!" Storm shouted louder than she meant to before she and Amber looked at each other and burst into a fit of laughter.

"So the hell are you fool!" Amber laughed.

The ladies sat there on the beach for the next two hours listening to music, sharing laughs, memories and edibles until they couldn't eat any more of them.

10

"DO I EVER CROSS YOUR MIND?"

-Brian McKnight

"Man, Storm, fucking around with your ass, I need some damn sleep. I'm so fucking high." Amber complained with her words slurring, slightly.

They were finally making it back in the house after they had laid on the beach for hours enjoying as much sun and sand as they could.

"Stop complaining... ain't no one tell your ass to try and keep up with me eating all those damn edibles."

"I wasn't trying to keep up... them shits were tasting good as fuck. I forgot they had weed in them, until now."

Bursting out laughing, Storm shook her head at Amber. "We have about three hours before we need to be getting ready to go. Go ahead and get a quick nap in."

"Oh, thank God!" Amber exclaimed, all but running to the room that she was occupying.

Stripping out of the minuscule clothes that she had been wearing, Storm prepared herself for a shower before she laid down for a quick nap.

Quickly going to her SiR *Pandora* station, Storm grabbed her portable speaker out of her bag before heading to the bathroom and running the shower water.

Not even five minutes into her shower, there was knocking at the bathroom door.

"Leave me alone, please and thank you!" Storm shouted over the music and water, hoping that whoever it was would take heed to her request. However, she didn't quite get her wish.

The gush of cold air that entered the bathroom told Storm that whoever had been knocking on the door, didn't respect her wishes. Choosing to ignore the person who had invaded her privacy the same way that they had ignored her, Storm continued singing her heart out with the music, dancing and singing.

Twenty minutes later, after she was sure that she had gotten every crevice on her body cleaned, Storm stopped the water and pulled back the curtain to find the surprise of her life.

"What the fuck!?" Storm screamed, closing the shower curtain to shield her body with her head sticking out of a hole that she had created with the shower curtain and the wall. "What the fuck are you doing here? How..."

With a smile on his face, Luck got up from where he had been sitting on the toilet bowl with Storm's towel in hand. "Why wouldn't I be here? My wife is here." Handing her the towel, Luck backtracked to the sink and leaned against it while his eyes stayed fixated on Storm.

Blowing out a breath of frustration, Storm closed the shower curtain so that she could quickly dry off before flinging back the shower curtain and stepping out of the shower with the towel wrapped around her.

"I'm gonna kill this girl." Storm muttered with Erin on her mind. Storming from the bathroom to her bedroom, she sat on the bed while looking at Lucky like he had three heads.

"What do you want, Luciano?"

"For you to come home."

"That's not going to happen, so if that's all..." Storm said, standing up.

"Storm..."

"Luck," Storm cut him off, moving to the door to open it for him when Luck grabbed her arm in an attempt to stop her.

"Don't touch me!" Snatching away from Luck, Storm twisted around to face Lucky so that he could see the seriousness in her words. "Please understand something... just because we had sex last night, it does not mean that things are going back to normal. That shouldn't have even happened yesterday, but it did. However, while we're talking about yesterday, let's not forget that I walked in on you and another bitch in my home too yesterday. What would make you think I would come home? Because the dick was good?" Storm waited to see if Luck would answer her but seeing that he stayed quiet, she continued. "Well, it wasn't that damn good. So no, I will not come 'home'". Storm said making air quotes around home. "Shit... if you ask me, I don't have a damn home. So again, if there is nothing else, I'm tired and would like to get some rest."

There was so much that Luck wanted to say in response to Storm, but he knew that right now wasn't the time. It was too soon... he knew it when he called Storm back to back and she didn't answer, when he reached out to Erin, even the whole time he made his way to the house Storm and the girls were staying in. However, it still didn't stop him from coming over there. Now, he wished he had gone with his first mind... to give Storm her space.

"You are right, Storm... I haven't given you a reason to want to come home. I'm gonna fix that..." With that, Luck walked out of the door Storm held open for him without another word.

* * *

"WHAT ARE YOU WEARING TONIGHT?" Erin asked, standing at the entrance of the room Storm was occupying during their stay. Storm was laying across the bed scrolling through Instagram; after Lucky's appearance, she hadn't been able to settle and fall asleep. She was pissed with Erin for more reasons than one, but the main reason was because she was meddling. If Erin knew nothing else, she knew that Storm was adamant about not wanting to be bothered with Luck. Yet, that hadn't been a deciding factor before Erin told him where they were.

"I'm not sure yet... I grabbed a few items from the house before I dipped out last night. I'm gonna try a few items on and see what speaks to my spirit."

"Uh huh... you trying to make sure you give that nigga Luck wet dreams tonight, huh?" Erin joked with Storm as she made her way into Storms room and sat on the bed.

"Nah... actually, I've already seen him even though I didn't want to." Storm said, looking Erin directly in the eyes.

"Storm..."

Raising her hand to stop the bullshit excuse she knew was going to leave Erin's mouth, Storm closed her eyes and slightly shook her head.

"Imagine my surprise, I'm standing in the shower, enjoying my music and shit and then someone knocks on the bathroom door. The only other people staying here are my cousin and sister so of course I'm not thinking that I would get out of the shower and find that man sitting on the toilet seat. I mean, it's not like I told him where I was staying... and it's not like I didn't tell you that I didn't want to talk to him. Hell, I've only been ignoring his calls all day. Why would I ever be forced to see and speak to someone that I vehemently said I didn't want to speak to?" By the end of Storm's statement, her voice was elevated, she had sat up so that Erin could better hear and see the frustration that had festered in Storm over the past two hours while she lay awake in her room thinking about the position she had been placed in.

"Storm, I'm sorry."

"What does that change?"

Storm had found comfort being somewhere that she knew Luck would never find her at. Now that he knew where she was, there would be gifts and more pop up visits to satisfy his selfish agenda. Forget the fact that Storm had also told him she didn't want to be bothered with him at the moment also.

"I was trying to help... you guys love each other, and I didn't want to see you guys demise over a misunderstanding."

"If you wanted to help, you should have minded your business. That would have been the best help you could have offered." It didn't make sense to correct or dignify the second half of her statement with a verbal response but in her mind she laughed. *Demise over a misunderstanding... yeah right.*

"I'll give you that, Stormie. I should have minded my business. I apologize for that and I promise it'll never happen again. I was dead wrong for that."

Storm wanted to say more, but the fact that Erin had owned up to her mistake, apologized and promised that it would never happen again was enough to make Storm shut her attitude down. This was their girl's trip and she wouldn't dwell on things that had already happened and couldn't be changed.

"I accept your apology... but this is not to happen again. Next time, I won't be as forgiving. Let me deal with my life, my marriage, my husband and my problems on my own and in my own time. If and when I need your assistance, I'll ask you... I always do." Storm said before laying back down on her bed and trying to get comfortable again.

"You got it and again, I apologize." Erin said before standing up and making her way out of the room.

As soon as her room was free of Erin, Storm rolled over on her back and gave her attention back to Instagram. Luck had posted a recent picture of him with a fresh haircut and Storm was feeling some kind of way.

For the first time in a long time, she couldn't say that she felt secure with where she currently stood in her relationship with Luck. Luck's pop up had awaken some feelings in her that she had been fighting off and now, she didn't know exactly how to deal with them.

Things had taken a left turn somewhere and she didn't know how they were supposed to redirect their relationship. Storm was hurt behind a lot and she was having a hard time getting over it, no matter how much she tried.

She missed Lucky though... she missed Los Angeles, she missed her house, her husband... she just wholeheartedly missed the way things used to be.

Her and Lau rushing home to be there with dinner ready when Luck made it in for the night. Even her riding out with him all day so that he could attend meetings and interviews. As much as Storm used to complain about having to do all of that, she would give anything to go back to that at this moment.

Almost an hour later, Erin was back at Storm's door screaming for her to wake up and start getting ready for the party they would be attending shortly. Storm wasn't sure of when she would have fallen asleep, but surely, she had passed out.

Once Erin was sure that Storm was awake, she strutted back to her room to finish getting ready herself. Storm laid around for a few more minutes before she decided to get up and get to it. Her first step of business was to make sure that her bedroom door was closed and locked because she was sure that sooner or later, one of the girls would be making their way to her room.

Feeling in the mood for some good music to get her night started, Storm scrolled to No Name's album *Room 25* and pressed shuffle. Going to her closet, she pulled out two of the three outfits she had been thinking about wearing and laid them across her bed before pulling out the shoes she was pairing the outfits with.

After brushing her teeth and washing her face, Storm went to the drawing board and got started putting her makeup on.

An hour later, all of the women were dressed to impress, standing in the living room taking shots before they walked out the door.

"We look the fuck good!" Amber shouted, admiring Storm, Erin and herself in the floor length mirror that stood in the living room. Dressed in a red BCBG Andi Lace Dress with a pair of nude Jonatina Christian Louboutin Sandals, Amber was every bit of classy and sexy and she knew it. Erin stood beside her in an Aidan Mattox Sequin Paillettes Cap-Sleeve Mini Dress that fit her like a glove and a pair of Balenciaga block heels with the logo on them. She had been unsure what to wear but it didn't show in her outfit at all. She looked like she had just stepped off of the runway.

Storm had decided to show up and show out being that she knew Luck would in attendance. She wanted him to see what he had and had lost in the same breath... even if she wasn't sure that they were done for good just yet. Dressed in a A.L.C., Kiera Belted Crepe Long-Sleeve dress that accentuated every curve her body held, Storm was feeling herself. The plunging neckline and concealed hook front gave her the sexy, yet business look she was going for. Pairing it with a pair of Vince Heath Cross Strap Sandals, she was flawless.

After taking over fifty pictures and turning off all the lights in the house, the ladies exited the house making their way to the car that Storm had waiting for them.

"So, are you excited to see Luck?" Amber asked, still unaware that Luck had been to the AirBNB earlier in the day.

"Why would I be excited?"

"Because your fine ass looks like that." Amber replied making Storm blush before she laughed.

"Well... when you put it like that." Storm said causing all three ladies to laugh.

"Let me call Ma really quick and check on Autumn before we make it to the party."

"I can't believe Steven's ass refused to watch her while we came on vacation."

"Yeah, his childish ass thought he was stopping someone's show. I bet you he is fuming where ever the fuck he is."

"You haven't spoken to him since we been here?"

"Hell no... I wish the fuck I would." Amber said drawing confused looks from Storm and Erin. Before they could comment on it, Storm's mom answered the phone.

"Hey Mama, how are you and the girls doing?" Amber asked, switching her tone up completely.

"Oh, really?" Ambers tone switched once again making Erin and Storm look at her.

"When was that?... How come you didn't call me?... Oh, okay. No, it's no problem, Ma... alright, talk to you later."

Hanging up the phone, Amber didn't bother telling the ladies what was going on and she completely ignored their questions asking her what was wrong as she muttered obscenities under her breath.

Putting the phone to her ear once again, she silently waited for whoever she was calling to answer. After a few seconds passed, Amber pulled the phone from her ear and cursed some more before dialing the number again.

"Who the hell are you calling?" Storm asked from the passenger's seat.

"Your stupid ass brother took Autumn from your mother's house without informing me after telling me he wouldn't watch her. Now this dumb motherfucker won't answer the phone. I swear I'm about to catch a case."

When Steven didn't answer again, Amber went to her text messages to send him a very nice text message while Storm picked up her phone to call him. After the phone had rung three times, she was sent to voicemail just like Amber had been.

"Ohh, he doing it like that?" Storm was shocked that he hadn't answered the phone for her. That was generally unheard of. There had been times when him and Am were in the middle of having sex and he would still answer just to make sure she was okay.

Doing like Amber had just done, Storm hung up the phone and tried calling Steven again. Once again, her call was sent to voicemail only after the first ring this time.

Going to her message's app, Storm composed a quick message to send to Steven. *'Why the hell aren't you answering your phone? Are you okay? Where is Autumn?'* Sending it, Storm watched the message go through and then delivered appeared before read and the time replaced it. Storm sat there watching her phone waiting for the three dots appear, but they never did.

The rest of the ride was a quiet ride. Amber was in her feelings, pissed off because Steven was playing games and Storm didn't quite know how to feel. She was hoping everything was okay with Steven, but she was still gonna fuck him up... regardless of if he was okay or not.

When they arrived, Amber did everything she could to get back in the mood to party and enjoy herself, but she was failing miserably. After walking around with her face scrunched up for twenty minutes, Storm dragged her to the bar for a few shots.

"You gotta snap out of this funk. I know you're pissed with Steven but we're on vacation... I need you to pull it together. He's throwing a temper tantrum, not answering the phone because he's tight you're out on vacation without his ass. If nothing else though, we know Autumn is safe. He won't allow anything to happen to her, you can bet your life on that. Now throw these shots back so you can snap the hell out of it. Shit, you just met Puff and your ass looked like you were meeting the grim reaper instead." Storm rambled on shoving two shots at Amber.

After monitoring her to ensure that she threw the shots back, Storm ordered two more rounds of shots for Erin, Amber and herself and then the two of them walked them back over to the couch where Erin was sitting holding their spots.

Once the liquor was coursing through Amber's body, she was back to her usual self. When *Nice For What* came on, Amber jumped up and started singing and dancing, pulling Stormie and Erin up with her. The three of them danced and sang the song like Drake had wrote it just for them. When the song ended, the three of them remained on their feet dancing and singing to the music

"Don't look now, but Luck just entered the backyard." Erin whispered to Storm, pretending like she was fixing Storm's dress.

Pretending like she was still dancing; Storm did her two step in a circle until she was facing the direction that she knew Luck would be in. It was like Storm's energy had attracted Luck because the minute she had turned around and laid eyes on him, he had also laid eyes on her.

Her breath got caught in her throat, her movement seized, and her heart rate increased as she admired the man that she had married over five years ago. Making his way over to her, it was like Luck had tunnel vision. There were men and women alike who kept trying to get his attention, but he paid them no mind. His only concern was the gorgeous brown woman dressed in white who had taken his breath away, too.

When he was in a close enough distance to Storm, he enclosed her in his arms before giving her a kiss on her forehead. "You look stunning," he told her with so much emotion that it passed from him to her.

"Thank you, so do you." Storm returned the compliment to him, meaning every word she said.

Taking advantage of the fact that they were in public and he knew Storm would never let outsiders into their world, he leaned in for a kiss.

With a smile on her face and through clenched teeth, Storm told him "you are pushing it, nigga." before giving him a kiss.

Turning to Amber and Erin, Lucky smiled bright and wide pleased with his accomplishment before releasing Storm and giving them both hugs and kisses.

"How long have y'all been here?" He asked, smelling the liquor pouring out of their pores.

"For about 45 minutes to an hour now," Erin told him being the only one to respond to Luck.

"Y'all having a good time? Did you introduce them to Puff?" Luck asked, looking over at Storm who was unsure exactly what to do. She didn't want to let on that there were some problems in her marriage right now that still needed to be worked out to the world, but she also didn't want Lucky taking advantage of the moment by making it something it was not.

"Yeah, they met him... anyway, you should go and make your rounds. Don't be rude, there are so many people here checking for you."

Chuckling, Lucky shook his head up and down, knowing that although Storm was worried about the business, she was also trying to move him away from her and he couldn't do anything but respect it.

"You're right... let me go and say what's up to everyone, I'll be back." He told them with finality before walking away from the three of them.

"Bitch, you're cold." Amber joked before she went back to dancing and singing with Erin. Storm stood there watching Luck's back as he maneuvered through the crowds of people giving him daps, hugging him and more.

"Let's go take some pictures." Storm said, snapping out of the daze she had been in.

11

"I CHANGED FOR YOU..."

-Jaheim

*B*y the end of the night, all three of the women were pissy drunk and had enjoyed themselves to the fullest. Amber was having a hard time walking in her heels as they tried to make their way to Luck's car. With all of the liquor that the three of them consumed, he refused to allow them to get into a cab. Storm and him had gotten into a small spat because she refused to get in the car with him. Even in her drunkenness, she refused to have another night like the one she had with him the night before.

"Uh!" Storm huffed once her butt had hit the passenger's seat and she was no longer on her feet. Her feet were on fire, but she still stood by not taking your shoes off in public. According to her, it wasn't "ladylike", and she made the ladies stand by it too when they were all together.

"Oh, my goodness!" Erin exclaimed in the backseat once she was seated and had her shoes off. She loved hanging with Storm but she hated the no taking the shoes off in public rule that Storm implemented whenever they went out. Erin swore by the Solemates Purse Pals Foldable Travel Ballet Flats that she constantly purchased from the drugstore every time she saw them. To her, it was nothing to pull a pair out of her oversized purse and replace her shoes with them. She didn't care if she looked different from the way she left the house, she just cared about being comfortable. "My feet feel like they are crying right now." She stressed, pulling her left foot up on her lap and caressing it with as much force as she could stomach.

"Y'all always wanna be cute and shit wearing them uncomfortable ass shoes. Better get y'all some flats or some shit." Lucky voiced, changing gears and taking off into the wee hours of the morning.

"Slow down, you know how curvy this road is, Luciano and mind your damn business. Don't no one want to walk around looking like a little ass girl or an old ass lady with flats on." Storm fussed with him causing Luck to smirk.

This reminded him of old times... when things were good between the two of them. He could recall plenty of nights when Storm would be drunk, and he would be the designated driver while she fussed with him about his speed even though he was going under the speed limit.

Taking his foot off of the gas slightly, he allowed the car to naturally slow down. Deciding to just allow the car to cruise and enjoy the moment, Luck reduced the speed some more and turned the music up a little bit and enjoyed the ride with his wife beside him and his sister and cousin-in-law behind him.

Twenty-five minutes later, they were pulling up to the AirBNB that the ladies had rented for their stay. Turning the car off, Luck got out and proceeded to open the everyone's door and help them out of the car.

Once they were all out, Storm turned to Luck to thank him for the ride. "I guess we'll see you at the BET Awards in a few days." Storm said, causing Luck's eyes to furrow.

"You don't want me to walk you guys in?" Luck asked, confused.

"We're good... we're here already. Thank you for the ride." Storm said, turning around and grabbing Amber's arm to help her walk to the front door in her incapacitated state.

"Damn... you're doing it like that, Storm?" Luck said from behind her. He was stuck in the same place unsure of exactly what to do. His ego was bruised... he had never experienced this side of Storm, not like this. It was like she couldn't get away from him fast enough whenever she was around him.

"What do you expect, Lucky? Shit ain't kosher between the two of us. You know it and I know it, so we aren't going to carry on like it is. So, yeah... I guess I am doing it like that." Storm told him and then walked away.

Anger coursed through Luck, but he could only be mad at himself. So, he did the only thing he could do at that point... get back in his car and head home with his tail between his legs.

"Y'all won't believe this nigga." Amber fumed as she made her way into the living room where Erin and Storm were laid out on the couch, watching *Impractical Jokers.*

Thanks to last night's party the three of them were drained and they had no plans to do much today besides resting for tomorrow's BET awards. Tonight though, they were hitting up World On Wheels as they had an event planned for BET weekend as well.

"What happened?" Erin was the first to ask, sitting up from

her comfortable position to observe Amber who was making her way to them while looking down into her phone.

"Look at this." Amber responded, handing her phone over to Storm whose hand was already outstretched. Leaning over so that Erin could see the phone also, Storm pressed play on the video that Amber had pulled up and waited for them to view it.

In the video, the ladies could see that Steven was at a club. Whoever was recording the Snap showed him sitting on a couch and a female sitting on top of him, dancing extremely provocative. Upon further inspection of the video, they could see that the two of them were actually fucking... in the club.

Steven and the woman were so into what they were doing, they didn't realize that they were being recorded. After realizing what was going on in the video, Storm handed the phone over to Erin and stood up to offer some comfort to Amber. She could see the hurt and distress on her face. Even though Amber talked a good game, Storm knew what it was.

"It's really over." Amber said, more to herself than to Storm who was slowly rocking her back and forth and rubbing her back in a soothing matter. Involuntary, tears began cascading down Ambers face. She had been trying to contain her emotions. Trying not to be weak, not to cry over the same thing she had been crying over for years... infidelity, lost love, disappointment. Yet her she was, crying once more because once again, she had stupidly given her heart back to the person who had broken it repeatedly doing the exact same thing each time. This was her breaking point. She was tired.

"I'm so sorry, baby." Storm replied to her.

Unsure of what to say to Amber, Erin sat there, phone in her hand watching the video over and over in disbelief. Steven had really lost all of his marbles and this video was proof of it. He was carrying on like he didn't have a whole wife... *What is he thinking?*

Erin kept thinking to herself. She wanted to step off and call him and give him a piece of her mind but what good would it do?

"How did you get this?" Erin asked, disgust evident in her voice, wanting to know if Steven even knew that this video was in existence.

"Someone recorded it on their snap and then sent it to me." Amber was able to get out through the liquid frustration and pain that she was currently experiencing.

"How do you want to move forward?" Erin asked, ready for whatever at this point. Family or not, Steven was dead ass wrong and she was not backing him on this one.

"I'm gonna carry on like I don't know anything until I find a place. I already know he won't leave... I gotta do it for myself, not even for Autumn."

"It's gonna be hard to be in that house with him everyday sis without letting on that you know."

"I know..." Amber whispered after sitting on the couch quiet for a while, sandwiched between Erin and Storm.

"You guys can move in with me." Erin suggested after minutes of silence engulfed them, allowing them to each live in the sorrow that was pouring off of Am.

"I appreciate the offer, but no, I can't. If he knows where I am, he's going to be popping up and in my space way more than he is with me in the same house as him." Amber knew the shenanigans he would carry on with... this wouldn't be the first time she left him, just the first time she stayed gone.

"When we get back, we can start apartment hunting for you, get you out of there as soon as possible."

"Yeah, I don't wanna catch a case." Am said, meaning every word she had spoken.

After more silence had filled the women, Amber spoke up once again. "You know what's crazy? I'm not even mad at him for doing what he's doing. I'm mad that he won't just tell me what he really wants. He's playing with my emotions... with my mind. Acting like I'm bugging when I know what I feel... what I see. The least he could do is give me the respect of knowing that this isn't what he wants anymore. I could respect that. Would it hurt? Yeah, but I wouldn't be looking stupid or feeling stupid."

"I completely understand..." Storm assured Amber, and she did.

"We gotta get out of this house... what do y'all wanna do?" Erin asked, deciding to change the subject.

"Whatever we do, there will be no drinking involved. I'm still trying to recover from last night." Storm admitted. She had been nursing her hangover since she'd opened her eyes this morning and here she was hours later with a hangover still brewing.

"Well, I need a drink." Amber declared.

"No, the hell you don't! You know you're an emotional drunk." Erin stressed.

"Right, I don't want to spend the day explaining to people why you're crying and cursing them out." Storm co-signed.

"Fuck y'all." Amber laughed, getting up from her spot on the couch and making her way to the room she was occupying. "I'm gonna go find me something to wear today. Y'all figure out what we are going to do... just make sure I can grab a drink or two wherever we go."

"Yeah the fuck right..." Storm mumbled under her breath causing Erin to laugh before getting serious.

"Can you believe Steven?"

"Nope... he's corny as fuck for that. He knows how much Amber loves him. He knows how much she's sacrificed for him... for their family and their life together. He's selfish. Only thinking about himself. Brother or not, I'm not fucking with him behind that. He's dead ass wrong."

"I'm feeling the same way. For months, he's been swearing up and down that Am was just bugging when all along, she was right on point. Had me thinking she was bugging by how hard he was going to convince me."

"Same... even though I knew she wasn't bugging."

"Do you think she's really going to leave this time?" Storm and Erin had seen this scenario more times than they could remember. It always started like this... Amber would find out that Steven wasn't being faithful, and she would leave him for a while but she always wound up right back with him.

"She's gone. He really lost her this time." Storm could feel it. Amber meant what she was saying and there was nothing that Steven could do to reverse it. It was really over.

"Damn."

"Yep, he made his bed..." Storm said, standing up and stretching.

"Now he's going to have to lie in it." Erin finished Storm's sentence before getting up and following Storm down the hall to their rooms.

TWO HOURS LATER, the ladies were finally making it to the spa appointments that Stormie had made for them last minute. Thankfully, she had a good rapport with the facility otherwise, the ladies would have had to find something else to do for the day.

"This place is beautiful!" Erin commented on the interior of the building they had just entered. Storm had booked the ladies a CBD massage each along with facials, manicures and pedicures at the Wi Spa—one of the best spas in Los Angeles.

"Yeah, this place is stunning. I love those chandeliers." Am commented, looking up at the ceilings and hanging crystal chandeliers that adorned the foyer.

"This is one of my favorite spots. Luck brought me here one year for our anniversary and I've been coming ever since." Storm commented as they stopped at the desk to get checked in and to obtain their keys for their lockers.

After going through the motions and getting undressed, they finally found themselves in the room they would be occupying for their massages. Decked out with glasses of wine and comfy towels wrapped around them that would soon be placed on the hooks provided for their full body massages, they already felt calm from the ambiance of the room of they were in... even before receiving their massages.

"Now I see why your ass loves LA so much, I'm starting to love it too."

"Yeah, I've been at peace since we stepped off the place." Erin co-signed.

"Girl don't let this little vacation fool y'all. There are times when Los Angeles is nothing but stress also. Wait until you have to go to the bathroom really bad and you're stuck in bumper to bumper traffic. Shit, I keep a gallon bottle in my car for those moments." Storm admitted before putting her hand over her face to hide her embarrassment.

"Well when you put it like that," Amber said, causing the three of them to laugh.

"I appreciate y'all..." Amber spoke up after the laughter had died down.

"Am, you don't have to..."

"Yes, I do. Here we are on our girls' trip that we've been dying to take for only God knows how long, and my life is crumbling right from under me. We've been saying how much we need a break for years now... especially me. Even though I've been trying to be a good sport, I'm struggling to hold it together. Yet you guys haven't complained or made me feel any kind of way behind it. Instead, y'all are dedicating the time that was supposed to be dedicated to yourselves... time that should be getting invested in y'all mental health and you guys are investing it in me. Neither one of you have to do this for me. I appreciate you both so much."

"We do it because we love you, Amber. You are family and family never get left behind. Imagine Storm or I getting upset because life has you fucked up. What kind of women would we be to leave you hanging like that? You never have to thank us for making sure you're okay. As family, that's what we're supposed to do. We've always done it and we always will." By now, Erin was battling the waterworks.

She knew all too well what it felt like for life to be falling apart around you and people expecting you to be moving like everything was okay. She remembered what it was like having to hold back tears and pretend she was okay because of a fear that no one would understand. She had experienced it when she found out her first love had been murdered and then again when she found out that she was pregnant. She would never put that weight on Amber just like Amber nor Storm let her wear that weight alone. Even when she up and moved to Atlanta, they were constantly making sure she was okay, visiting when they could, sending money for food and clothes when they were sure she needed it. They had always been her ride or dies, just like she would always be theirs.

Feeling like there was nothing more for her to say, Storm lifted her glass in the air with her eyes locked on Amber's briefly before locking them with Erin indicating to them to lift their glasses as well. "To sisterhood... may we always remain as we are, may we always remain best friends, may we never leave one behind. I love y'all."

They repeated after Storm and then finished off their glasses before laying on their stomachs on their designated massage tables and taking off their towels. For the rest of the day and well into the night, the ladies enjoyed their alone time, nursing their mental health and their emotional health as well.

12

"I CAN BE YOUR NOAH, YOU CAN BE MY WIZ"

-Method Man

"Storm, are you almost ready? Luck said he'll be here in less than ten minutes." Erin screamed through the locked door separating them from seeing the creation that was Storm.

"Yeah, I'll be out soon." Storm shouted back, completing the finishing touches on her make-up.

Dressed in a black Oscar De La Renta tulle gown with gold embroidered flowers, Storm was stunning. The plunging neckline, full skirt and the gold accents on the gown brought out a glow in her that was out of this world. Paired with a pair of Jimmy Choo, Aveline 100 black sandals with an asymmetrical grosgrain mesh bow and a clear wristlet with black and gold accents on it, she was to die for.

Storm had decided to wear her hair in a twist out with the left side of her hair pinned to over to the right side. Her makeup was light, a natural look with dramatic bold eyes. Her jewelry was minimal, a simple gold choker, the matching bracelet, gold diamond studded earrings and her engagement and wedding rings. Simple yet elegant.

Looking herself over in the mirror once more, she gave herself a smile, satisfied with her look. She wanted tonight to be a winning night for Luck. Regardless of what was going on between the two of them, she would never deny his talent and the amount of work he put in. As hard as he worked, he deserved it, she had to admit that.

Grabbing her cell phone, she headed out the door ready to meet with the girls in the living room. When she made it downstairs, she was shocked to find Luck already there, sitting on the couch waiting for her.

Hearing Storm's heels on the ground and the ooh's and ah's from Amber and Erin, Luck stood up and turned to see Storm. Breathing halted, heart pounding and eyes misting, Luck was at a loss for words. Storm looked like a breath of fresh air; she was exquisite.

"Are you going to say something or are you just going to stare at me?" Storm asked with a smirk on her face. The responses she was getting were the exact responses she was looking for. She had spent the entire day planning her look and preparing for the night and it looked like she had bodied it.

"You are captivating." Luck said, pride emitting from his being. He was always proud of having married Storm. She was the best thing that had happened to him outside of Lauryn and although he didn't always display that when dealing with her, he knew it.

"Thank you," blushing, Storm casted her eyes down to the

ground in front of her before he eyes shot back up at Luck. "You look amazing yourself."

Luck was dressed in a navy Emporio Armani Two-Piece Wool Tuxedo with Satin Peak Lapel with navy and gold Gucci loafers. Under his tux jacket was a white button up shirt with a navy-blue bow tie that had gold trimming around the bow. In his breast pocket was a gold handkerchief with hints of navy-blue dancing through it. Luck had a fresh cut and line up with his hair in its natural curls, sitting on top. Like Storm, his jewelry was minimal. In his ears were 1 ct. Diamond studs sitting in 14k yellow gold, on his wrist was a Hublot Big Bang diamond watch and on his left hand sat his gold and diamond wedding band that he never removed.

"There are other people in the room... damn, y'all acting like it's just y'all here." Amber said causing Luck, Storm and Erin to laugh.

"You look beautiful, Sis. Erin, you too." Luck said turning to look at the two of them.

"Don't hate heifers... he likes what he sees but you both look beautiful. We're about turning heads all fucking night." Storm playfully boasted.

"I love what I see." Luck replied, once again putting his attention on Storm. Taking a step towards her, he put his hand out for her and when she handed her hand to him, he pulled her close and wrapped his arms around her. Feeling Storm tense up slightly, Luck loosened his grip on her.

Not wanting to kill Luck's mood, Storm wrapped her arms around him and hugged him back, tightly. This night was for him, she told herself repeatedly. She didn't want anything to ruin it... not even her bruised ego or indecisive mind.

Pulling back from the hug, Storm looked up at Luck, hesitating before giving him a kiss. A kiss that started out as a peck, but that Luck took advantage of and turned into a full on make out session.

"Alright now, motherfuckers... y'all gonna cut that shit out now." Amber said, causing everyone to burst out laughing.

"Damn sis, you don't have to be a hater." Once Luck had pulled away from Storm, he gave Amber his undivided attention. Arm still wrapped about Storms waist, possessively.

"Ain't no one hating but you are pushing it. This is a girl's trip. You're infiltrating that right now even if you are our ride."

"Damn, that's all I am?" Feigning hurt, Luck released Storm and placed a hand to his mouth and a hand to heart.

"I'm just being honest..." Amber said, leaving out of the room, making her way to the front door. "Can we go now? I didn't get this pretty to stand here and watch y'all make out."

Following Amber's lead, Erin, Storm and Luck made their way out of the door behind her.

With traffic, it took the four of them damn near an hour and a half to make it to the Staples Center where the BET Awards were taking place. As their driver was pulling up to the red carpet, Storm, Erin and Amber were finishing up their makeup touch ups.

"We ready?" Luck asked as he prepared to step out of the door that the driver was holding open for him. Paparazzi with their cameras ready were already taking pictures and shouting Luck's name.

Looking at Erin and Amber for confirmation, she shook her head, "yeah, we're ready."

Stepping out of the car, Luck turned back around and reached in for Storm. Taking his hand, she stepped out alongside of him, a smile plastered to her face, already knowing what to expect.

She had given Erin and Amber a pep talk this morning explaining to them everything they would be enduring when they made it to the red carpet. She knew that although they were probably excited about their first red carpet, they had never experienced anything like this before. It was going to be an experience that they would never forget and Storm made sure that they were prepared for it in advance.

Next, Luck reached in for Erin who was sitting closer to the door than Amber. Stepping out of the car dressed in a champagne and gold colored Bariano embellished patterned sequin strappy maxi dress, she looked stunning. Her hair had been straightened and cut into a blunt bob that accentuated her round face. Large diamond studs sat in her ears and a medium sized gold flower adorned her neck and stopped about two inches above where her chest met her dress. On her wrist was a gold wristlet and on her feet were gold sequined Jimmy Choo sandals that she had gotten from the flea market that Storm had dragged them to earlier this morning.

Her makeup was barely there, a natural look per se. Erin hated wearing makeup and if she had the choice, she wouldn't have worn it today. Storm and Amber had cursed her out something terrible though when she told them that she wasn't planning on wearing make-up.

Lastly, Luck reached back into the vehicle and grabbed Amber's hand to help her out of the car. Feeling like a million dollars, Am stepped out of the car with her smile on and her head high. Whereas Storm and Erin opted to wear long gowns, Amber decided that she was rocking a mini dress.

In a black dress that stopped a little higher than mid-thigh. There were silver chains draped around the dress randomly and patches of purple, green and pink. Her BCBG shoes were similar to her dress. There were zippers adorning the material around her ankle and the black on her shoes were a reflector of all of the colors in her dress, depending on how you looked at the shoes.

In her hand was a black and silver clutch, even her fingernails were painted black to go with her ensemble. Her hair was straightened, reaching the middle of her back. Her makeup was out of this world, she had gone for a dramatic and smoky eye with a dark burgundy and black ombre' lip. Everything about her was on point.

Once all of the women were out of the car, Luck grabbed Storms hand and they made their way to the red carpet. Majority of the pictures were taken with just Luck and Storm... a few with the girls as well. From the outside looking in, there was no way anyone would be able to tell that there was trouble in Storm and Luck's relationship. For a second, even Storm and Luck forgot that there were problems in their relationships. Up until it was time for the group to move along the red carpet to media.

The first person they encountered was Kara, Luck's friend. Her makeup was flawless... whoever her makeup artist was had done such a good job covering up the scratches and bruises that had covered her face after Erin and Amber had finished with her.

Comforted by the cameras and people surrounding them, Kara put on her petty boots. With a smile on her face, she welcomed Luck and Storm to her. "Lucky, congrats on your nominations tonight. You look amazing." Lust clouding her vision as she looked him over from his head to his toes, completely disregarding Storm's presence.

"Thanks, but the truth be told, my wife is what has me looking amazing. Without her on my arm, I'd be a regular joe." Looking down at Storm and tightening his grip on her hand, he willed her to let him handle the situation. Although he knew that Storm wouldn't make a scene here, she had never been one for the disre-spect. It would be nothing for Storm to curse Kara out right here with no regard for where they were if she kept trying her luck.

He knew Kara thought the cameras would save her, but Luck knew different.

"Oh yes, your wife. Hi Stormie, you look nice!" With a fake smile plastered on her face looking as if it burned her tongue to even get those words out.

Void of a smile, Storm looked Kara in her eyes, debating what to say if anything. "Really?" Storm asked, her signature devious smile gracing her face. "And you look like a hater. Now thanks for your congratulations and your great eye of my fine ass husband, but we've got to move along now." Storm said dismissing Kara with a smile.

Without further word from either of them, Storm and Luck started to move down the long line of media waiting for them and countless others to grace them with their presence.

After they had spoken with the final media outlet, the group made their way into the Staples Center. The second cameras were no longer present, Storm snatched her hand from out of Luck's.

"Storm..." Luck started but was cut off by Storm muttering under her breath.

"Un-fucking-believable." Picking up speed to get as far away from Luck as she could, Luck decided to let her cool off before he tried to do any damage control.

"What the fuck was that?" Amber asked the second she had caught up to Storm.

"Luck's side chick is media... I already know that fucking interview is about to be on every outlet, but I don't give a fuck. She's lucky I didn't black her other fucking eye."

"We can always catch her later..." Amber suggested looking for someone to beat on to help her get rid of some of the frustrations she was feeling from dealing with her situation with Steven.

"Fuck her, it isn't worth it. She could have this nigga if she wants him." Storm was furious with Luck, with this entire situation. More than anything though, she was furious with herself. For a second, she had allowed herself to forget. Forget everything that had transpired and just keep it pushing was what she thought would happen. She thought that they would be able to move past some of the bullshit they had encountered but running into Kara here made her reevaluate that thought.

If there was nothing worse than Luck dealing with another woman, it was him dealing with a woman that ran in some of the same circles that they ran in. Although Kara wasn't famous, her being media meant that she would be permitted into a lot of the same events they would be permitted into. Today was a prime fucking example.

Finding her way to the bathroom with her girls trailing behind her, Storm needed a breather. After a quick pep talk with the ladies and reminding herself that they were there for Luck... to see him receive his first award, she was ready. Regardless of whether they were on good terms or not, she hadn't missed an important moment in his life as of yet and she didn't plan on missing one now.

Once Storm was seated next to Luck and Erin and Amber had taken their respective seats on either side of them, Luck grabbed Storms hands before giving it a squeeze and leaning into her.

"I apologize for that, Storm." Luck whispered. "I…"

"Don't. I don't want to talk about that right now. I'm trying to stay in the festive mood right not, that'll ruin it." Shutting down the conversation with those few words, Storm smiled at him and gave his hand a squeeze to ease his mind, as well.

Three and a half hours later and two won awards, the group of four were inching their way out of the award show with the crowd of people who had also been in attendance.

"Y'all hitting up the after party?" Luck asked the second they had made it out of the Staples Center, and they were headed to his car.

"Hell yeah!" Amber and Erin said at the same time.

"Y'all fiending." Storm told them laughing at their synchronicity and speed.

"It's our last night, we're trying to get wasted and have a good ass time."

"Y'all are leaving tomorrow?" Luck asked, looking exclusively at Storm, shocked that she hadn't said anything to him about it yet.

"Yeah, our flight leaves tomorrow around 5 in the afternoon."

"Why didn't you say anything? When are you coming back?" He asked, hopeful. He was hoping that they would be here longer so that he could do some more work overtime to get his wife back.

"Luck!" His name was called from behind him. He knew the voice before he even turned around. Groaning, he turned around, praying that Kara wasn't on any bullshit. The last thing he needed was for Storm to get pissed off when she was in such a good mood.

Stopping midstride alongside of Lucky, the ladies turned around also, wanting to know who was calling him. When they spotted Kara briskly walking towards them, they knew it was about to be some bullshit.

Trying to pull her hand out of Luck's, Storm was annoyed and fed up with Kara and Luck at this point. Clearly there was more to the situation than Luck claimed and if there wasn't then someone needed to tell Kara that. Until she was aware of that, Storm wanted no parts of Luck or getting her marriage back on track.

"Wassup, Kara?" Luck made sure to hold Storm's hand tighter. He wanted to be sure that Kara got the picture. He had never told her or led her to believe that they were doing anything more than just hanging out. Hell, on countless occasions, he had talked about Storm and his relationship. Telling her how much he loved and missed his wife.

Actually, prior to the day that Storm had walked in on them, they had never even gotten past hanging out in public places out of respect for his marriage. That day had really been a mistake... a huge mistake. The fact that she was playing like she didn't know who Storm was and wasn't showing any respect for her as well, was pissing him off.

However, there wasn't much that he felt he could say. Being that Kara worked for the press, he understood that she could easily put whatever narrative out that she wanted to. People would believe her, it was a part of her job, regardless of whether it was true or not—people would eat it up.

"Well, I wanted to congratulate you on your wins tonight..." Kara said, knowing that wasn't all she came to talk to Luck about.

"This woman cannot be fucking serious." Storm fumed, still trying to get her hand free from Luck.

"Thanks... is that all?" Luck asked, already turning around without waiting on her response.

"Umm, no... I was hoping I could celebrate with you."

"Oh, this bitch has balls, balls." Amber said, immediately stepping out of her shoes and pulling her earrings out of her ears.

"She's only doing what Luck has set the stage for... I'm sure he would love to celebrate with you, baby. Y'all enjoy y'all night." Storm said, successfully pulling her hand out of Luck's this time.

"Storm, I don't want to celebrate shit with this bitch... I'm here with you." Luck was fed up... clearly Kara could see that he didn't want any parts of her, but she was study trying her luck.

"You were here with me, but you aren't anymore. You're free to do as you please, Luciano. Again, enjoy." And with that, Storm started moving again. She wasn't sure where she was going or how she was getting there, but she was definitely getting the fuck away before she lost her cool and put her hands on this woman and Luck.

"Storm, you gonna really allow her to ride off into the sunset with your husband?" Erin asked, confused. She was ready for war yet here Storm was walking away, handing Luck away.

"Have you seen Luck check her once since we been here, and she's been disrespecting me?" Storm asked, causing Erin and Amber to think about it. "Luck is one of the most disrespectful niggas I know but I haven't seen that side of him yet when it comes to her. He's condoning this shit."

"She's right, he hasn't tried to check her once." Erin said, thinking over all of the situations where they had to interact with that woman.

"That's what we're here for... we can check her. Storm, you keep letting this bitch try her luck with you and Lucky. You're really going to allow her to be the reason why shit doesn't get right with you and your husband? You're giving her your power."

"Listen, I'm not you, Am. I'm not fighting for no nigga, husband or not, when he's blatantly showing me what it is. I've already played myself enough when it comes to this man and this situation. This entire fucking week that we've been here, he has had the opportunity to put her in her place. He hasn't... not in front of us and clearly not behind closed doors. She isn't carrying on like this for no reason. I'm a lot of things but stupid is not one of them. She is acting like that because he has given her the battery needed for her to move like that. I'm done wasting time with him."

"Wow... tell me how you really feel." Amber's feelings were hurt from Storm speaking her truth although that was never Storm's intent.

"Get out of your feelings, Amber. This has nothing to do with you and everything to do with the fact that I expect you both to stand by me and my decision to walk away. Regardless of whether you agree or not. Clearly, neither one of you can do that, so I'm out. Y'all can stay and go to the after party with his trifling ass, but I'm good."

Pulling her phone out of the small bag she carried, Storm went to her Uber app and ordered herself a car.

"Storm..."

"Luck, don't even bother."

"All this time you been getting in my ass because you said that I've been running, well now, I'm here. I'm here trying to work this out and you're running. How can we fix anything if you aren't even trying to stay long enough to get anything right?" There was venom in his voice, like he had the audacity to be mad.

"Hold on, let me get this clear... when I wanted to get it right after you *thought* I had fucked up, you weren't with it. Now that *you've* fucked up, you want to work shit out, right?" Storm asked, hand on her hip and her head cocked to one side. Luck had a lot of fucking nerve.

"So, we doing tit for tat?" He knew he couldn't win this one... his only resolve was to play on Storm's conscious. Try to make her feel guilty for the shit he had done.

"You needed time, right?" Storm refused to give in to Luck.

When he refused to answer, Storm decided to answer for him. "Now I need time..." Storm told him just as her Uber pulled up.

Turning around, Storm left him, Am and Erin standing there with Kara not too far away from them as she jumped in her Uber. She was done playing with Luck, he had to feel her now.

"YOU DID THIS TO US..."

-Tammy Rivera

"What are you doing?" Am asked, walking into the room that had been designated Storm and Lauryn's room for the duration of their stay.

The ladies had only returned from their trip to LA the night before. The entire ride back had been tensed between the three of them with Storm giving the ladies the silent treatment majority of the time. The only time she answered them is if she had to... otherwise, Storm kept her headphones in the entire ride with her music blasting. Granted, there were some things on her mind that had her preoccupied, but she still wanted to be clear that she wasn't feeling either one of the ladies.

By the time they had made it in from the after party the night before, it was daybreak. The only thing the ladies were able to do when they got in was pack, take a shower, eat and head back out.

They had to drop Storm's car off at her and Luck's house and then catch an Uber to the airport. Their whole day had been consumed with traveling. By the time they made it back to NY they all just wanted their beds.

Being that she was so exhausted by the time they made it back, Storm decided to just pick Lau up today being that she was also going to pick up the keys for the apartment she had solidified yesterday while sitting in the airport waiting on her flight with the ladies.

"Packing..."

"Well I can clearly see that, but why? I thought you were staying here for a few more days before heading back."

"Since everything that happened in LA, I decided to stay in NY a bit longer... indefinitely, actually. I found an apartment and we move in today."

"You did all of that without telling Erin or I?"

"I didn't want any input... I know where you and Erin stand with the whole Luck and I situation. I didn't need to hear y'all tell me how much of a mistake I was making or how y'all wouldn't do it if y'all were me."

"Woo, hold up, Sis... regardless of how much I think you should work shit out with your husband, I'm *always* team you. Don't do me like that... If you would have told me that you were planning on staying in NY because you felt it was best for you and Lau, I would have helped you look for an apartment. Hell, as hard as I've been looking for a place since seeing that video, we could have found one for the both of us and been roommates."

"I'm sorry, Am." Storm said finally breaking the wall that had been up around her for the past day and a half, taking a seat on the bed. "I just feel like no one is concerned with my feelings. Everyone is worried about how Luck feels and the state of my marriage, but no one seems to care about the hurt I'm experiencing. I know we're all family, but right now, I just need someone to back me and tell me that I'm not wrong. That I'm right to stand up for myself, even if it is against Luciano."

Shaking her head, Amber understood where Storm was coming from. Although the ladies thought they were being supportive of Storm and her choices while still giving her advice, she realized just how much they hadn't been supportive to Storm at all.

The last thing she ever wanted to do was to make Storm feel that way. Storm had stood by her side through some shit that should have had her questioning Amber's sanity and loyalty, but Storm held it down. Her loyalty was unmatched if you asked Amber.

"I apologize if I haven't been supportive of you and your feelings, Storm. I thought I was doing the right thing by advocating for your marriage. You know I would never do anything to make you feel like what you are going through doesn't amount to anything."

"I appreciate that, Am..." Storm said, still in her feelings. It had been a hard few weeks having to hear the feedback she constantly heard from Erin and Am. Everyone seen her as being the difficult one, not giving her marriage an opportunity to get right. They didn't realize that she was trying to protect herself. The last thing Storm wanted was for her to give Luck another chance to let her down because that was exactly what he had done. Hell, her entire circle had let her down.

There were so many times that she had gone to bat with her own brother for Amber and yet, when it was Amber's turn to return the favor, she chose him over her.

"Storm..."

"I'm good, Am. Listen, I'm gonna come back for the rest of my things, I need to go and grab Lau from ma's house then I'm heading over to our new place. I should have all of my things out by next week." Storm said not really in the mood to hear any other apologies. She needed time to herself with her baby for now.

"Don't do that... don't close yourself off from us, Storm."

"Listen, I just need time. I need some time to get myself together and situate my thoughts. When I'm ready to talk, I will be sure to let you all know. For now, I just want to be left alone." With that, Storm grabbed a few of her bags that she could carry with no problem and made her way out of the room and down the stairs while Amber sat on the bed trying to understand what the hell was going on.

"LAURYN!" Storm shouted through her mother's house the second she had the door unlocked and open. She was excited to be reunited with her baby girl after a week of not seeing her. Neither Storm nor Lau were used to that and Storm definitely didn't want to get used to it.

"Why are you yelling in my house?" Storm's mom asked, walking out of the living room and into the foyer of her home.

With a smile on her face, Storm approached her mom and gave her a big hug and kiss before responding.

"I miss my baby girl. Where is she?" Storm asked as she stepped out of her shoes. Pam was a stickler for shoes in her house. She always preached to them that she had no way of knowing what anyone stepped on or in while outside and because of that, she made everyone take their shoes off at the door.

"She's upstairs watching television. Now, tell me all about your trip... how was it?" Pam asked, she was hoping that Storm and Luck had a chance to make things right between the two of them. Pam loved her son-in-law, and she knew that he was Storm's equal. She was praying that this little misunderstanding wasn't going to be the end of their relationship.

"It was nothing like I expected." Plopping down on the love seat, Storm pulled her feet up beside her and got comfortable before she gave her mother the full run down of everything that had transpired while her, Erin and Am were in LA.

"Wow... so he had that woman in your house?" Pam asked again for clarity. She had heard everything that Storm had said, but she had to be sure.

"He sure did... then he allowed her to disrespect me on more than one occasion. It took everything in me, Ma. I guess people think that because you become a celebrity by some people's standards that you never lived before that. I swear, God was with her."

"Or maybe God was with you... he knows that you have too much to lose just like he knows that husband of yours is about to get a call from his favorite mother in law."

"You're his only mother-in-law, Ma."

"Yeah, and I'm going to be his only mother in law in this lifetime."

Rolling her eyes, Storm finished her conversation with her mother before going upstairs to find Lauryn.

"Hey baby girl!"

"Mommy!" Lauryn exclaimed as she jumped up and went skyrocketing to her mother. Although Lau loved being with her grandmother, she missed her mom.

"I take it you missed me?" Storm asked, with a smile on her face just as wide as Lau's. Seeing Lauryn made her forget everything that had transpired over the last week. She loved that Lauryn had the ability to do that without her even having knowledge of it yet.

"Duh! I missed you a lot. Are we going home now? I miss daddy too." And just that quickly, everything was back in clear view.

"No, baby... actually, that's something that mommy wanted to talk to you about. We're going to be moving back to NY. We move into our new place today."

"Yay!" Lauryn yelled louder than she needed to. "When is daddy getting here?"

"Daddy isn't moving with us, Lau. Mommy and daddy are going to live separately. That means you'll have two houses to go to now." Storm told her trying to get her to see the brighter side of things. The smile and excitement that had been emitting from Lauryn only seconds before had dissipated just that quickly.

"I don't want two houses though. I wanna go back home and live in our house with daddy." Lauryn cried. Storm knew this would be difficult for Lauryn but she was hoping that it would be a quick transition.

"What's the matter with her?" Pam asked, standing in the doorway of the room that Storm and Lauryn were currently in.

Blowing out a frustrated breath, Storm closed Lauryn in her arms and rocked her back and forth in a soothing manner before turning to look at her mother.

"I told her that we're moving to NY... we move in to our new place today."

"You're staying out here?" Shock evident on Pam's face. Her and Storm had sat downstairs talking for damn near an hour and she hadn't heard a word about Storm moving back here.

"Yeah, I'm not going back..."

"Storm--"

"Ma, not right now. I've dealt with enough of the Luck support group to last me a lifetime. I'm staying and that's that." Storm said, turning back around so that her back was to her mother. She was over it... she couldn't get anyone to understand her side to save her life.

"I play a lot of games, but disrespect has never been one of them, Storm. Turn around and look at me while I'm talking to you." Pam fussed, hand on her hip. When Storm turned around to give Pam her undivided attention, she continued. "Now you can get mad all you want but understand that we are advocating for what we think is best for you. You want to live in your feelings, you be our guest and do that. However, you will not dictate our opinions. We are on the outside looking in, we see that the both of you are being stubborn and spoiled as hell... both mad because y'all can't have your way the way you want it. We're trying to help you save yourself from an unhappy, boring and miserable life because we all know that Luck is your happiness. But if you want to give your husband away behind some miscommunication, be our guest."

With that, Pam turned away and started making her way back to where she came from, leaving Storm with a lot to think about. Stopping midstride though, Pam turned back around and looked at Storm. "Oh, and make sure you text Amber and Erin before the day is out. Whatever your vendetta is with Luck has absolutely nothing to do with them. You are walking around here mad at the world when you need to take a closer look at yourself."

Storm sat there for over an hour, still rocking a now sleeping Lauryn while she thought about everything her mother had said. After pondering on it for a while longer, Storm brushed it off. She had every reason to be upset and she was standing by that. However, her mother was right about her needing to reach out to Erin and Am. Taking her phone out, she went to their group chat and typed three simple words knowing that all would be forgiven afterwards. *'I love y'all.'*

14

"SPIRIT TESTED BUT STILL UNDEFEATED"

1 month later

"*What are you doing today?*" Amber asked the minute Storm had answered the phone.

"*Nothing really, I wanna do some shopping for Lau today being that school starts in a few weeks.*"

"*Okay, well you know I'm always happy to spend money.*"

"*Me too!*" Erin chimed in, exposing that Amber had called Storm on three-way.

Laughing at their silliness, Storm climbed out of bed and went to the bathroom to begin her morning routine. "*What time do y'all want to meet?*"

"*I'm ready now,*" Erin informed Storm and Am.

"*I'm ready also.*"

"*Well, y'all can try that again. I'm just climbing out of bed so I'm going to need y'all to give me some time.*"

Teeth sucking could be heard as Storm imagined that they were both shaking their heads at her. Amber was always up at the crack of dawn just like Erin but if Storm didn't have to be up early, you could bet your last dollar that she wouldn't be.

"You got an hour. We will be outside in exactly one hour... don't have us waiting."

"Yeah, yeah, yeah! I'll see y'all then."

Hanging up before either lady could threaten her anymore, Storm finished up on the toilet and then turned on the shower. While she waited for the bathroom to fill up with steam, she went to the sink to brush her teeth and wash her face. Holding her phone in her hand while she brushed her teeth, she found herself at the Instagram app. The second her timeline had refreshed; she was staring at a picture of Lucky. She could tell that he was at the house that the two of them had previously shared. Dressed in a pair of distressed jeans with a fitted T-shirt on that showcased his muscles, Storm couldn't help the storm that brewed in her heart.

To anyone else looking at the picture, they would probably think he was chilling, enjoying life and shit. However, she could see the truth in his eyes and his posture. He was just as stressed and unhappy as she was. It looked like he hadn't slept in days, his eyes were dark and heavy, and his complexion was uneven. Not to mention, Storm could also see that he had lost some weight. Clicking on his name to be directed to his profile, she waited patiently for it to finish loading.

Under normal circumstances, she tried to stay away from his page but being that Lauryn would be with him for the next two weeks, she would be checking his page much more often that she would regularly.

Going through all of his pictures, she took her time to read through his captions and even some of the comments. Feeling slighted by some of the things people had said, she rolled her eyes at them wishing she could dislike them. The ones she liked, she tapped the red heart next to them.

Seeing that he had posted a picture of him and Lau earlier in the day, Storm liked it before commenting a bunch of heart eye faces before she screenshotted it.

Deciding to post it to her own story, she wrote, "What Love Looks Like" before pressing send and exiting the app. Turning on her Lyfe Jennings Pandora station, she placed her phone on the counter before stepping out of her clothes and getting into the shower.

Despite things being rough between Luck and her, they were still married. More than that though, they were family. Two adults who shared a child. He could piss Storm off from there to Mexico and there would still be love between the two of them.

Standing under the water, all Storm could think about was how much things had changed and how they were still changing. Even with the current state of their relationship, Storm still couldn't honestly say that they were done. She would love for them to be able to work out their problems, but the ball was in Luck's court. She refused to chase him. His running was the cause of this, so he would have to figure it out.

At exactly 55 minutes after Storm had gotten off of the phone with Am and Erin, she was stepping out of her building to wait for them outside. Even though 9 times out of 10, they would arrive late, Storm still needed to be on time. To her surprise though, when she stepped out of the building, they were already parked in front.

"I can't believe this shit!" Storm said to herself loud enough to be heard before looking up at the sky as she ran to the car with her arms shielding her head.

"What the fuck is wrong with you?" Amber asked from the driver's seat.

"Pigs gotta be flying... I just know you aren't here on time!" Storm dramatically stated, causing laughter to erupt from the ladies as she made her way to the back seat.

"I guess that shows you how much you know!"

"Oh please, this is the first time you've *ever* been on time for anything." Storm teased. There was a running joke between the three of them. Normally, Storm and Erin would tell Amber that events started an hour earlier just to make sure that she made it on time. Hell, even her clients knew not to show up on time unless they wanted to be upset.

"Anyway," Amber started as she pulled out into traffic. "Let me tell you about your brother and your cousin."

"Uh oh, what his dumb behind do now?" Pulling her seatbelt across her chest, she listened for the click before giving Amber her full attention.

"This motherfucker stayed out all night the other night."

"He what?!" Erin and Storm exclaimed simultaneously.

"Where the fuck was he at?" Storm asked.

"I hope bookings." Erin said feeling every bit of pissed that she knew Amber was feeling.

"I don't know... the nigga keeps on telling me he fell asleep at his homeboys house, but I know that's bullshit."

"How do you know that?" Storm asked, praying that her brother had been at his homeboy's house and not laid up with a woman who wasn't half of what his wife was.

"Because I called all this niggas friends and the ones I couldn't reach, I called their women. Every single person said the same damn thing... they hadn't seen Steven and didn't know where he was."

"Damn..."

"My point exactly."

"This lying motherfucker gotta be really feeling this bitch. He's really ready to risk it all."

"I been knowing he was, Storm... what other reason would there be for all of the bullshit that I've endured these past couple of months?? Shit, he can't be feeling her too much, fucking her in clubs and shits. He clearly doesn't respect her."

Shaking her head, Storm didn't have a response for Amber. Clearly Steven was up to something no matter how much he continued to deny it to her and Erin.

He still didn't know that they had seen the video with him and shorty in the club and sworn to secrecy by Amber, they couldn't say anything about it. So, they played along with him like they believed him... no matter how hard it was.

"I can't go through this shit anymore, y'all. I really thought we were past this cheating shit a long time ago. I would have never married him had I known he would still be on this shit." Amber stated trying to refrain from crying.

"I can't believe you still haven't said anything to him about that fucking video. I would have gone crazy the second I walked in the house." Erin said, not believing the strength and will that Amber was displaying. It would have been WW3 had she been the one in Amber's shoes.

"I have to... if I don't keep it to myself and decide to bring it to him and this nigga lies to me, I'm going to jail." Amber declared.

"I feel you on that, Sis. I would have to two piece his shit for you." Storm said, feeling her blood boil with just the thought of it. Had this been the situation with her and Luck, that nigga would have known what he did the minute she peeped. However, she respected Amber's decision because she knew how much she hated a liar.

"Well, I can't say what I would do because my ass doesn't have a man and I haven't had one in about five years but baby... I be with the shits when it's one of y'all so I know I would be with the shits if it was me."

"Say that shit!" Amber said laughing, thankful for the laugh because she was ready to be engaged in a full-on bawl just now.

"Well, are you still planning on moving out?" Erin asked, even though she knew exactly what Amber was planning to do. Hell, had it been her, she would have been gone but Amber had really tried to stick it out.

"I'm out... I'm taking Autumn and I'm getting the fuck out of dodge. Besides our birth certificates and socials, I'm not even taking any of the shit in that house. He can remember us by it."

"I'm really in no position to say much because as you can see, I'm here in New York and Luck is still in LA but I think you should at least talk to Steven first before you bounce. Get some clarity about the situation."

"I don't think so. I don't need him lying to me anymore than he already has. I know what I need to know."

"I guess there's nothing else for us to say then... when are you planning on moving? Why you still there? We been back for more than a month already and you still there?"

"I'm having a hard time finding a place, I think I'm going to stay with my mother."

"Out of all of the places you and Autumn can stay, our houses included, you would rather go to your mother's house? You two can't get along longer than ten minutes." Erin said, upset that Amber had to subject herself to not being in the comforts of her own home along with Autumn. She had every intention of running down on Steven the minute she was away from Am. He had another thought coming if he thought he was getting away with the bullshit he was pulling.

"That may be true, but if I come to either one of your houses, y'all know Steven will be there every single day and all day at that. At least at my mother's house, I know he will stay away."

"True..." Storm said. "Damn, you and Steven been together for as long as I could remember. I can't believe it's really coming to this."

"I can't do it anymore... I hate that it's come to this too but I'm tired of fighting, now. For as long as I could remember, I been fighting women for him and fighting him for him all while fighting me for the stupidity. I'm done."

"I don't understand. He has a daughter now... he's gonna have hell to pay when Autumn is old enough to start dating." Erin prophesied.

"The sins of the father..." Storm agreed while Amber sat in the front seat thinking about what they were saying.

This was going to be a drastic change for her. For more than 10 years, Steven had been her everything. Having to even think about leaving him was tearing her apart but she was determined to leave this time and stay away while she was at it. Steven had proven that he didn't love her the way he said he did. If so, she wouldn't be feeling the way she was currently. Nor would she have to uproot her child and herself from their home because of the shit he was doing.

Amber knew this was going to be a drastic change, but she was ready for it. She had no choice but to be ready for it, this was her reality now.

FORTY-FIVE MINUTES LATER, the ladies were arriving at the outlets in Long Island. Their first stop was the bathroom to release their bladders so that they could shop until they dropped.

"What store are we starting at?" Stormie asked the girls as they stepped out of the bathroom and into the hallway.

"I don't care, as long as I can max out all of Steven's cards, I'm good. He's gonna pay for what the hell I'm feeling. And losing his family isn't enough."

"Well, Adidas and Nike are over here... we can start there with getting the kids some sneakers and little sweat suits for the fall."

"I like the way you think, Erin!" Amber chuckled

"Summer left too fast." Storm complained. The main reason she was down with moving to LA when Luck first said they were going was because of the weather. She hated the cold, the winter, the snow.

"Who are you telling? It's back to school already."

"I'm not ready." Storm confessed. "This will be the first time that Luck won't be here to see Lauryn off to her first day of school. Not to mention I'm in New York while he's in LA... he won't be able to help her with her homework and participate with her schooling."

"I mean, he could do all of that if you would take your ass back home." Erin told her, not in the mood to hear Storm complain.

"That's not happening... not anytime soon at least. He needs to fix this."

"He tried, Stormie... you weren't with it."

"When did he try?"

"The whole time we were in LA!" Amber jumped in the conversation.

"No, that was him feeling guilty. I don't understand... Did you guys forget that I waited two whole weeks for that nigga to come home before I finally left Los Angeles? Then, I was gone for a whole two weeks with no call from him. Not even to see how Lauryn was doing. Had it not been for him posting on Instagram, I really wouldn't have known if he was alive or not. Not to mention, when I finally go back to the house him and a bitch are sitting on the couch I picked out, in the house I designed for him, our daughter and myself. Both of them half-dressed and shit?! No, him begging a little isn't fixing shit. If he really wants his wife back, he'll figure out how to make it happen. Until then, he's on his own."

Shaking her head, Erin decided to say what her and Amber had been thinking all along. "You're stubborn as fuck yet you're always claiming that he's so stubborn. How can you miss someone daily, love them and want to be with them, yet you refuse to answer their calls most of the time? You won't even meet up with him with Lauryn so y'all could have a family day or something. Anytime conversation between the two of you gets to talking about y'all reconciling you ending the call or ignoring his text messages. You need to make up your mind. It's either you want your marriage or you don't. You've been so evil to him, but you expect him to continue jumping through hoops to make you happy and feed your pride. Keep it up, you gonna mess around and lose your husband playing all these games." Erin told Storm, giving her something to think about while they finished shopping.

When Storm made it home from her day out with the girls, she was drained. Not just physically from all of the shopping and walking they had done, but emotionally and mentally from the conversations they had as well. The things that Erin had said were true, but she didn't know how to be any other way with Luck right now then the way she was being.

His constant running anytime things didn't go his way and him not even trying to hear what she had to say in regard to the surgery. She understood it was an emotional thing for the two of them to deal with, but it was something they were supposed to deal with together. His running didn't permit that. What it did was show Storm that it was his way, or no way and she didn't like that.

If she could be honest, she was beyond hurt and yes, her pride was bruised. Despite everything they were facing, she still believed that some things were just completely off limits. If there was one thing she believed wholeheartedly, it was that Luck would never step out on their union. Regardless of whether they were on good terms or not, that was never supposed to be an option. Other people dealt with those problems, not them. Yet, she had walked in on him and another woman, proving that they weren't exempt from anything.

Even if Luck and that lady weren't doing anything when she walked in, the evidence was there that they had already done something and that was more than enough for her. There was no way she would ever go back to that home to live in after that.

Getting undressed, Storm climbed in the bed and buried herself under the covers. This was where she wanted to stay until her heart no longer hurt... until she could face the music that maybe, just maybe, Luck and her weren't as perfect as she thought.

Three hours later, Storm was up from her nap, feeling like shit. For the past few weeks, she'd been so stressed behind her situation with Luck that she'd literally made herself sick.

She was just recovering from the flu... something she hadn't had in years. She seemed to keep a migraine as of lately and had been dizzy more times then she could count. She was kicking herself in the ass for allowing the stress of this situation get to her like that, so she had made a vow to dead all of that.

Getting up, Storm headed to the bathroom first to relieve her bladder and brush her teeth before she went to make herself something to eat. Searching through the fridge and cabinets, Storm couldn't decide on what she wanted.

Deciding to go out for a night alone, Storm headed back upstairs. Throwing on a pair of sweatpants and a hoodie, Storm grabbed her favorite sneakers, her black and white Nike Prestos. They were some of the most comfortable sneakers she had ever purchased in her life.

Deciding to eat clean since she was still getting over the flu, Storm opted for a vegan restaurant named Toad Style. She loved their fries and the sunshine burger they offered. Making sure to grab her Kindle on the way out, Storm grabbed her keys and headed to the car with food on her mind.

Fifteen minutes later, Storm was arriving at the restaurant and searching for parking. When she found it, she headed in the restaurant grabbing a menu, even though she already knew what she wanted and had a seat at the wooden table seated across from the register.

After reviewing the menu and verifying that she didn't want to try anything other than what she was used to, Storm got up and made her way back to the register, leaving her kindle on the table she had just abandoned to let others know that it was where she was sitting.

"Hi, can I get the sunshine burger and a small fry? Also, do you guys have the rainbow cookies?"

Taking a look at the small refrigerator behind the counter, they smiled before telling Storm that they did have them and putting the rest of her order into the computer.

"Can I have three of them?" Storm asked, figuring that she would eat one now and then save the other two for when she needed a midnight snack later on.

After she paid for her food, Storm reclaimed her seat at the table and opened her Kindle. She was in the midst of reading

'Crowned BAWSE: Getting Over Forever' by Sky EM. It was a good book that Storm was having a hard time putting down for long periods of time.

Just as Storm's food was ready, her phone was vibrating against the table. Looking at the screen, Storm's face immediately broke out into a smile. She hadn't spoken to Lauryn since yesterday and she missed her.

"Hey baby girl! How are you?" Placing her food down on the table, Storm had a seat with her phone lifted to her face so that Lauryn could see her just like she was able to see Lauryn.

"Hi Mommy! Where are you?"

Was the first question Lauryn asked Storm. *"I'm at Toad Style, see?"* Turning the camera around so Lauryn could see her food, she kept the camera trained for a while before turning it back on her.

"Aww man, I wish I was with you." Lauryn said, meaning every word. Since she had been introduced to this place, she loved it. Although she never really ordered anything more than the French fries, she loved the idea of them making their own ketchup.

Picking up a fry and putting it in her mouth, Storm continued her conversation with Lauryn until their conversation was interrupted by a guy who had just walked into the restaurant.

"Stormie?"

Looking up from her phone, Storm focused on the guy in front of her trying to figure out where she knew him from. Coming up with a blank, Storm gave him a slight smile and then returned to her call with Lauryn. The whole time she talked to Lau, the guy stood to the side of her table watching her, making her uncomfortable.

"Baby girl, let mommy eat her food and I'll give you a call as soon as I walk in the house." Storm said. Finally fed up with the guy, plus her food was getting cold.

Disappointment washed Lauryn's face which Storm immediately picked up on. "I promise, baby. I'm going to eat before my food gets cold and then I'm calling you right back. I won't even wait until I get home..."

The promise of her mother eating and then calling her back made her happy enough to agree with what her mother was saying. After they had hung up, Storm placed the phone in her pocket and opened her Kindle before getting started on her food.

"I apologize, I didn't mean to be rude, it's just..." The guy started, but seeing that Storm wasn't paying him any attention, he stopped.

Putting her Kindle down on the table, Storm put her focus on the guy in front of her. "Listen, not to be rude or anything, but I'm trying to enjoy lunch alone."

Holding his hands up like he was surrendering, he expressed to her that he understood, however, that didn't stop him from talking to her still.

"You don't remember me, do you?" He asked, like that would somehow make her magically remember.

"If I did, I would have said so by now, love." Storm was losing her patience. She really just wanted to eat and enjoy some time alone and this guy was making it hard to do.

"We met at..." The urge to throw up erupted in Storm before she could stop it and she jumped up from the table knocking it and her food over at the same time while trying to make it to the bathroom.

By the skin of her teeth, Storm made it to the bathroom where she emptied the contents of her stomach, which weren't much.

"Shit, are you okay?" The guy had followed her to the bathroom and was now standing in the doorway watching her as she cradled the dirty toilet that so many people had used for the door. With a splitting headache, Storm nodded her head and stood up before flushing the toilet and washing her hands.

"I gotta get out of here." Storm mumbled to herself. Pulling some napkins from the napkin holder, Storm brushed past the man who was still occupying her space. The table had been picked up, her food discarded and her Kindle on the table. Grabbing her Kindle, she made her way out of the restaurant.

"Can I at least get your number so we can touch base when you're feeling better?"

"I'm married, Sir." Storm said as she climbed in her car and started it before pulling off with lightning speed.

15

"ONE STEP AWAY FROM NEVER COMING BACK HOME AGAIN..."

-Tammy Rivera

"**M**y cycle hasn't been here since before fucking LA for the BET Awards." Storm admitted to Amber. "Bitch, that's damn near two months already. What the hell you been waiting on to do this?" She inquired as the two of them sat in her bathroom staring at the pregnancy tests, on top of Amber's bathroom sink, that they had picked up earlier from Dollar Tree.

"Truthfully?" Storm asked her even though she knew that Amber only wanted the truth. After she looked at Storm and rolled her eyes, Storm continued. "My fucking husband." It was officially six weeks since she had seen or spoken to Lucky about anything other than Lau. She had sent Lau to LA to spend some time with Luck for a few before he got busy with all of his press runs and shooting videos for the new album. So, lately, Lau was all they talked about... otherwise, Storm wouldn't be talking at all.

Two weeks ago, Storm decided that she would extend her trip in NY permanently as she didn't feel like there was much of a reason to return to LA. Having to deal with the mess of her and Lucky didn't appeal to her right now and she assumed that it didn't appeal to him either since he hadn't tried to do more than call her a few times.

There was no way she was going to continue to drive herself crazy; crying every night, not eating, and stressing herself out, when he was clearly out living his best life. So, she decided to stay in New York... indefinitely. Give him a taste of his own medicine. Maybe if he saw what it felt like to miss her, he'd understand what he was really losing.

"I can't believe it's been this long since the two of you have spoken about y'all relationship."

"Yeah, me either, but we better believe it." Hoping that the results had popped up to kill the conversation that the two of them were having, Stormie peeked over at the test.

"I knew it." Amber declared.

"Me too..." Storm had known for a few weeks now that she was pregnant, she just really wanted to find this out with Luck by her side.

"What are you going to do?"

"Make an appointment to make sure that this baby is not in my tubes."

"If the baby isn't in your tubes, you're keeping it... right?"

"Hell yeah, as long as Luck and I have been trying to have a baby."

"But shit is all fucked up between the two of you right now."

"No offense, but who gives a fuck? That don't have shit to do with *my* baby. We could get a divorce tomorrow; I'm still keeping my baby." Storm wished she would allow the situation with Luck to dictate whether she kept her child or not. Maybe in her young and dumb years, but definitely not in this day and age. Amber was crazy for even asking Storm some shit like that.

"Okay, I just wanted to make sure." Cutting her eyes at her, Storm grabbed the pregnancy test from the counter before dropping it into the garbage can and heading back to Am and Steven's bedroom with Amber following behind her.

"There was nothing to make sure of. With or without Luck, I'm having my baby. I'm a grown ass woman, fully capable of taking care of my two kids and myself."

"Say that shit, Sis."

Laying across the bed with Amber beside her, Storm thought about how different things were going to be this time around. When she was pregnant with Lauryn, Lucky was there, loving on her and making sure that she was good the entire time. Well, with the exception of when Crystal killed herself, but Stormie knew that he wasn't in his right mind at that time, so it didn't even count.

"STORMIE JOHNSON?" A week later, Storm and Amber found themselves sitting in Storm's old GYN office... the same GYN she'd had while she was pregnant with Lau. The second she walked in the office; nostalgia engulfed her.

The nurse was calling Storm's name from where she stood between the door and the frame while she looked down at her chart. Jumping up from where she had been sitting with Amber, Storm made her way to the nurse, sure that Amber was behind her.

After taking down Storm's weight, blood pressure, and asking her a few routine questions the nurse handed her a cup and directed her to the bathroom to pee inside of it.

Returning back to the room after handing the nurse the cup halfway filled with her urine, Storm waited patiently for the doctor.

"Are you worried?" Amber asked her after a few minutes passed with the two of them sitting in silence.

"A little, but I know that what's meant will be."

"True..." Their conversation was cut short by the doctor walking into the room they were occupying.

"Hi, Ms. Johnson?" She asked looking down at the chart that she had picked up from outside of the door on her way in.

"Mrs. Hi Doctor, how are you?" The joy in Storm's voice couldn't be ignored. Looking up at Storm, the recognition triggered, and the doctor broke out into a wide smile.

"I'm doing good, how are you? It's been such a long time." Hugging Storm, she showed her genuine happiness to see her.

"I'm good... here again." Storm joked.

Laughing, the doctor shook her head saying she understood before her attention was on Amber, sitting in the corner. "And who do I have the pleasure of meeting today?"

"Hello, I'm her sister. It's nice to meet you."

"Likewise." The doctor smiled at her. "What are we here for today?"

"Well, I'm pregnant but in the past, I've suffered from ectopic pregnancies. I just want to make sure this baby is in the right spot."

Shaking her head, she fingered through Storm's chart before putting her attention on her. "Okay, so you are definitely pregnant. When was your last cycle?"

Searching through her phone for the cycle tracker app, Storm told her the date she had last recorded.

"That would put you at about seven weeks along. We're going to do a transvaginal ultrasound and then we can go from there." Reaching over to a draw a few feet away from her, she opened it and pulled out a sheet. "I need you to get undressed from the waist down, I'll be back in a few minutes with the technician and machine."

Once she left, Storm stripped out of her clothes and laid back down on the table with the sheet placed over her lap.

Twenty-five minutes later, both ladies were walking out of the doctor's office with ultrasound pictures in hand and smiles on their faces.

"It would be now that shit is all fucked up between you and Luck that you would get exactly what you've been begging God for."

"Who are you telling? But I'm not complaining. Everything happens for a reason, right?"

"True." Was all Amber said as she sat in the passenger's seat with her head buried in her phone.

"Storm..." After minutes of silence between the two of them, Amber was finally interrupting it.

"Wassup?" Storm asked her with her attention still on the road.

"Pull over really quick."

"What? Why?"

"I need to show you something..."

"Pull over? Can't whatever it is wait until we make it home?"

"It could, but it's not going to..."

Doing as she asked, as soon as Storm was able to, she pulled over to the side of the road. "What do you need to show me?"

Handing Storm the phone, she saw that she was on Instagram looking at The Shade Room's page. Focusing her attention on the picture that she was showing her, Storm's heart dropped to her stomach. Scrolling down a little more so that she could read the caption, she felt the bile rushing towards her mouth.

"Looks like there may be some trouble in paradise... #Lucky is spotted out with another woman on what appears to be a date. According to sources close to the rapper, the two of them have been seeing each other for a few weeks. Well, #Roommates want to know, where is his wife #Storm? We haven't seen any post from him in regard to her lately, and she's completely abandoned social media. Anyone know what's going on?"

Throwing Amber's phone back into her lap, Storm quickly opened her car door and stuck her head out of the door before emptying the little bit of food that she had put in her stomach early that morning. Long after the food had left Storm's system, she was still dry heaving as Amber held her hair back out of her face.

Finally feeling okay enough to sit up and close the door, Storm reached over Am into the glove compartment and grabbed some napkins. She was crying and still feeling sick while battling thoughts of what to do next. Storm refused to call Luck and give him a piece of her mind... she felt like he should be the one to call her and straighten all of this shit out. Hell, he knew that the blogs had posted this just like Storm now knew.

"I'm sorry, Sis." Am whispered while she rubbed Storm's back in an attempt to comfort her.

"Sorry for what?" Storm asked her, finally feeling okay enough to pull out into traffic. "Luck did this shit to me... to us. Not you, you have nothing to be sorry for."

With nothing else to say, they drove the rest of the way in silence. Storm with a heavy heart and Amber with just the same.

"Do you want me to come and spend the night with you? I can hit Erin up and we can make it a girl's night" Amber inquired the second they made it back to Amber's house.

"No, I'm good. Tomorrow, my baby girl comes home, tonight, I just want to spend some time alone coming to terms with all of this." Inside, Storm was fuming. They were married, not just in a relationship. She didn't care what problems they were having; you don't deal with them by running... running away from home or running to the next bitch. Not to mention, how dare he publicly embarrass her like that. He knew that being a public figure meant no privacy...

"Well, what are you going to do now?"

"File for a separation, shit, I already have an apartment here... I might as well get comfortable with it."

"You really want a separation?"

"I didn't... but now, I don't have a choice. I'm not about to let him disrespect me and think shit is sweet. There are repercussions to everyone's actions, his included and he knows that."

"BURN SAGE, BUT KEEP THE ASHES

The energy is frequently high, let's keep the balance."
-KAI CA$H

a private call coming through Storm's cell jolted her from the nap she was currently enjoying a little bit too much. Her ringtone, that she could have sworn she had silenced earlier in the day, blared through the room while her phone vibrated across the nightstand it was currently sitting on. Reaching over from her position in bed to grab her phone, Storm quickly swiped her finger across the screen to answer the call before it was sent to her voicemail.

"Yeah?" She answered, completely disregarding the fact that her particular greeting wasn't professional. At the moment, she could care less, though. She was exhausted and looking to get back to sleep just as soon as the call was disconnected.

"A fucking separation?" Luck screamed through the phone the

second he heard Storms voice. Prior to her answering the phone, he had coached himself on what he would say when he had the chance to speak with her. He had the entire conversation mapped out in his head and yet, he had blown it the moment she answered the phone.

"Hi Luciano, nice to hear from you." Storm said, sitting up in her bed and rolling her eyes. Clearly, the sleep she thought she would be enjoying was out of the window.

"Don't fucking play with me, Storm! You filed for a fucking separa-tion?" Storm could hear the disbelief in his voice. Luck would have never in his wildest dreams believed that Storm and him would be dealing with the issues that they presently were.

When him and Storm met, she was a breath of fresh air, and all of these years later, she was still that for him. However, they were adults now and they had adult problems which couldn't always be worked out in a single conversation or over the matter of a day. Yet, he hadn't expected this.

"What did you expect, Lucky? You're moving like you're single anyway, right? Why should I hold onto something that clearly isn't mine?" Storm asked him to let him know that she knew about and was pissed behind the picture of him and that woman, floating around the blogs.

"So, let me get this straight, you filed for a separation behind some shit the blogs posted without even giving me the opportunity to speak my case?"

"Don't that sound familiar, Lucky? Shit, you left my ass without giving me a chance to speak my case." Storm chuckled at his audac-ity. *"But what case is it that you're speaking on, Luck? You have so many of them to speak on..."*

"Storm..." Luck started before stopping to give himself time to calm down. Storm took that as her invitation to keep on speaking.

"Don't Storm me... which case is it, Luck? The case where you are constantly running from our problems instead of talking about them? The case where you don't respect me enough to allow me to give my input on situations we deal with and have some sort of say in the final outcome? Or the case regarding you not coming home for over two weeks because you were having a temper tantrum."

"Yo, Storm," was all Luck was able to get out before Storm started speaking over him again to get her point across.

"Maybe, maybe it's the fact that I walked into my home and seen you with a woman that didn't look like me at all. Then, I go to the doctor to find out if my pregnancy is ectopic or not and how far along I am in my pregnancy, only to be blindsided when I leave of a picture of my husband and this same woman who had no right to be in my home nor with my husband in the first damn place. Which case would you like to plead, Luciano?!" Storm screamed, finally getting some of the things she was dying to say to Lucky off of her chest.

"You're pregnant?"

"That's all you heard? You didn't hear nothing else that I said?"

"None of that other shit matters, Stormie. You're pregnant?" He asked once again.

"Like hell it doesn't... all of that shit matters. It's the whole reason why your daughter and I are living in NY and you're living in LA. It's the reason why shit between the two of us haven't been straight in damn near three months. It's the exact reason I filed for separation and paid my rent for a year in a condo here in NY. Don't tell me that shit doesn't matter."

"Wait, what? You got a condo in NY? What the fuck are you talking about, Stormie? I thought you guys were coming back by the end of the summer. We're married... you aren't about to just move to another state over 3,000 miles away with my child and think that shit is okay." Lucky said further deepening the scowl that was on Storm's face.

"Oh, you got me fucked up." She exclaimed as she threw the

covers back and climbed out of bed. *"We were also married when you were out on a date with a bitch that isn't even a quarter of me. Or when she occupied space in my home... should I keep going?"*

"I wasn't out on no fucking date, man!" Lucky yelled back at Storm even though he knew he wasn't telling the truth. At this point, he was desperate. He would say anything if it meant everything between Storm and him going back to normal.

"You're a fucking liar... and there goes another thing you can add to the list." Storm said, shaking her head in disappointment. *"You know something, Luciano... a few months ago, I wouldn't have been able to fathom the thought that you weren't the man I've known for the last decade or so. But now, the disappointment doesn't even sting, it's starting to get easier to accept."* She said, making his breath get caught in his chest. He could feel that he was losing her, and he didn't know what he had to do to correct it, but he was on it now.

"Just keep something in mind while you do what you do... even in the court of law it's three strikes and you're out." Storm told him before hanging up the phone and throwing it back on the bed. Pacing back and forth in an attempt to calm herself didn't work fast enough for her. Storming off to the bathroom to relieve her bladder she couldn't help but to think that maybe everyone was right... maybe she played a bigger part in the state of their marriage then she cared to admit.

Even though she hated to agree, but maybe Erin was right. Maybe this had gotten as big as it had because of her stubbornness. She was just having a hard time with letting everything go and she wasn't even sure if she should let it go or not.

"Y'ALL NEED TO TALK, STORM." Erin stressed for the thousandth time that night.

All three ladies were in their pajamas at Erin's house with cups of wine, and a cup of tea for Storm.

After picking Lauryn up from the airport earlier, Storm and Lauryn headed straight to Erin's house where they were all having a sleepover—the adults and the children alike.

Cuddled up on the couch, the ladies were talking about Storm and Luck's phone call from earlier that day even though Storm would rather talk about something else. She had said everything that she wanted to say in regard to Lucky for the night but Amber and Erin weren't hearing it.

"Did you not hear me tell you both all about the conversation Luck and I had today? We talked already." Storm said even though she knew that wasn't what Erin was talking about.

"Cut the shit, Storm." Amber spoke up. "Do you want your marriage to end for real? Because if you don't speak up soon, you just might get that, regardless of if you're ready or not for it."

Taking a deep breath and releasing it dramatically, Storm unfolded her legs from under her as she sat up and placed her mug on the coaster. "Speaking truthfully, I don't know what I want... Of course, I don't want my marriage to end, I've seen forever with Lucky since I met him, but I don't ever see us getting over this. Too much has happened. Maybe this is what's best."

"Bullshit, the only reason you don't see reconciliation is because you want to hold on to that hurt and anger. And truthfully, not that much has happened. Let that shit go, sis... that's your husband for a reason."

"You are saying all of that but what's your excuse?"

"Oh, we are not the same and you know that. My marriage is over... there is no question about that. I won't lose sleep, cry or anything else about it. The most I might miss is the companionship but even that ain't shit if I'm being honest. You, on the other hand will lose your mind if some shit goes left between Luck and you." Amber said, stating the obvious. Storm would definitely lose her mind if a divorce was to happen between the two of them.

"I can't let this go though, y'all. Every time I think about Luck, I think about him leaving. Then, I think about walking into my house and seeing him sitting there with that woman... then the blog posts. Every time I think I can get over the last thing he's done, he does something else to make me hold onto it a little tighter."

"Well, express that to him. Y'all communication sucks, y'all need to fix that if this shit is gonna work between the two of you."

"I just need time right now. I think that the separation will be good for us. We need some time apart."

"Time apart? What about the two months that you two have already spent apart?"

"Clearly, it wasn't enough. Plus, that was time when I couldn't focus on me because I was so focused on him. I'm taking this time to focus on my kids and myself. If it's in the clouds for Luck and I, it'll work itself out the way it's supposed to."

"I hear you, sis. Just remember that you said that." Amber and Erin were tired of the back and forth. They had been dealing with this for only a few weeks now and already they were tired.

Although they loved them both, they were ready to wash their hands of the two of them and let them figure it out on their own.

17

"THE CHILL ME, THAT'S THE REAL ME. BUT WHEN YOU FORCE MY HAND, I GOTTA PLAY THE CARDS YOU DEAL ME."

-Fabolous

"*I miss you, daddy. When can I come back home?*" Storm was heading back to her room from the kitchen but hearing Lauryn on the phone prompted her to stop short at Lauryn's room door to listen to what she was saying.

Lauryn had been back home for a little over two months and had been giving Storm a run for her money. Lauryn was missing her father something terrible and she made sure to let Storm and everyone else know every chance that she got.

When school started, she threw a fit because Lucky wasn't there to walk her to her first day of school with her mother. When she was at school, she was always telling the teacher and her classmates all about her father. Whenever her and her mother spent time together the only thing she would talk about was her father and their home in Los Angeles. It was so bad that Storm had gotten angry with Lauryn a few times for being what Storm called "fresh" while trying to express her emotions for her father to her.

"No, I miss our house."

"No, we haven't gone to Uncle Steven and Aunt Am in a while. Since mommy got an apartment, they all come here... Mommy's in her room right now. She sleeps and cries a lot and she's always angry with every-one. I want to come home." Lauryn said before beginning to cry. Knowing that Lauryn had noticed the depressed funk that Storm had been in lately broke her heart. She didn't think Lauryn had recognized it but then again, how could she not?

Having heard enough, Storm pushed open Lauryn's cracked room door and made her presence known. Doing her best to keep a neutral face, she walked over to Lauryn's bed and sat at the foot of it.

"Hey beautiful," Storm said, with a small smile on her face.

"Hey mommy." Lauryn responded, using the sleeve of her night shirt to clean the tears from her caramel complexioned face.

"Can I talk to you for a minute?" Shaking her head yes, she told Luck that she would call him back before saying I love you and hanging up the phone.

"I first want to apologize to you. Mommy has not been herself lately. I've been in a funk and I didn't know that it was affecting you also. Going through changes with this new baby, the weather and season changing, missing our home and your dad are weighing on me also. You aren't alone with what you are feeling. I feel it too and I promise that I will make it a priority to make our experience here much better. Starting now.

Today, we're going to get dressed and then, we're gonna go and find you a costume for next week before going to the movies and dinner. How does that sound?" Lauryn's face lit up with that news. Jumping up from her seat and onto her mom with a huge smile on her face, she wrapped her arms around her and flooded her face with kisses.

"Yay!" Lauryn exclaimed.

Laughing, Storm was just happy to change the mood and make her baby smile. "I love you, Lau."

"I love you too, mommy."

"You better. Now, go and find you something to wear today and I will go and run your bath water." Getting up from the bed, Storm went to the hallway bathroom and started Lau's water. Leaning into the tub, she plugged it before heading back to her room.

"E, what are you and Damia doing today?" School had just started a few weeks ago and she hadn't seen Erin or Damia since. Storm had started showing a few weeks ago and had been confined to the house because she didn't want the blogs in her business and her picture all over social media. She had made it through her first trimester weeks ago and that had been her excuse for not telling the world all before time. However, now she wasn't quite sure how she would break the news to them. Things still weren't copasetic between her and Luck and she knew that the comments would be a whole lot of bullshit.

She wasn't sure if it was the weather changing or the pregnancy that had her depressed and lazy more days than not, but she was over it. Especially knowing how this was affecting Lauryn now. Today, she was breaking out of it. She knew that being away from home was hard enough on Lauryn, she had no intention on adding to her frustrations or sadness.

"Not a thing. We just finished doing our laundry and were just gonna stay in the house for the rest of the day."

"Well, let's change that. How about we do the movies and dinner tonight with the girls?"

"That sounds good... what kid movies are out right now?"

Pulling the phone away from her ear, she placed it on the speaker and went to her internet browser where she had Fandango already pulled up. *"Small foot, The house with a clock in its walls... and that looks about it."*

"What are you leaning towards?"

"Small foot... the other one has witches and shit in it. I don't fuck with that."

"Your punk ass." Erin laughed, but secretly agreeing with Storm.

"I'll be that." Getting off of the bed, Storm moved to her closet to find something comfortable to wear for the day.

"What time do you want to meet up?"

Looking at the clock on her wall above her TV, she saw that it was 12 p.m. Being that it was Sunday, she didn't want to have the kids out late. *"Well, the movie shows at 2:20 and 4:45. I think the 4:55 movie will be better. The movie only runs for an hour and a half so we can take them to dinner afterwards and still be home by 9."*

"Sounds like a plan to me. I'll see you soon."

"Alright, meet me on Court St at 4:20 so that we can get good seats and snacks before missing the previews."

"You and them damn previews." Erin hated the previews. It reminded her of commercials, and she hated those as well. Erin didn't even watch live TV because of the commercials. Either she recorded the shows and fast forwarded past the commercials or she caught it on Netflix or Hulu.

"Well, this was my idea... so previews it is." Storm said, sounding like the spoiled brat that she was.

"Bye, Storm." Erin said as she pressed the end button, leaving Storm holding the phone between her ear and shoulder with a smirk on her face.

Plugging her phone up to the charger and connecting it to her

Bluetooth speaker, she opened her Tidal app and pressed play on her Real Love playlist before throwing her phone onto the bed. Walking into the bathroom attached to her bedroom, Storm started her shower room before stripping out of her clothes. Standing in the mirror, she studied her body for a while as she sang along to Queen Naija's 'Medicine'.

'Swear I cannot win for losing,
I been out here being faithful.
I always got this on lockdown,
But that ain't been keeping us stable.'

AT FOUR AND a half months pregnant, she already had a very noticeable baby bump. She didn't remember showing this quickly with Lauryn. Rubbing her belly, she smiled at the life she was carrying inside of her. Everything in her body told her that she was carrying a little boy. This pregnancy was so very different from her pregnancy with Lauryn. Even though things weren't the best when she was carrying Lauryn, she was much happier than she was now.

Lau was her first child and even though she was scared, she was still excited. She wanted to know who Luck and her had created. This time around though, she wasn't feeling like herself. She was depressed and resentful... all feelings that she didn't want to pass on to her baby boy. Getting in the shower, she quickly got herself together while singing along with her music. When she was done, she grabbed her towel and wrapped it around her before stepping out of the shower and grabbing her mango and papaya scented shea butter.

Twenty minutes later, she was emerging from her bedroom feeling refreshed and fully dressed.

"Lau, let's go mama."

Seconds later, Lauryn was running from her room to the front door where Storm was already standing with the door open waiting on her. Being that they needed to be downtown in a few hours for the movies, Storm decided that they would go to the Party City at Atlantic Terminal.

"Can we take the train, mommy?" Lauryn asked knowing that Storm hated any kind of public transportation. However, because today was all about Lauryn, Storm agreed.

On the walk to the train, the two of them shared conversation. Storm was surprised at how advanced and in the loop, Lau was on the things going on between her and Luck. Making a mental note to not speak about her relationship woos with the girls in front of her any longer, Storm still felt like it was the perfect time to put Lauryn up on game.

"If you don't remember nothing else that I teach you over the course of your life, Lau, never forget this. You teach people how to treat you. If you allow people to treat you how they see fit, and you don't correct it then that's how they'll always treat you. The first time someone does something that you don't like, you correct it. Have a conversation with them regarding it and set boundaries with them. If they love you and respect you, they'll take heed to those boundaries and ensure that it doesn't happen again.

Now, if it happens a second time, then you have to leave them alone. Even if you don't want to, you have to make them feel it so that they know that you mean what you say. Do you understand me?" Shaking her head up and down, Lauryn indicated that she had heard what her mother said.

"Use your words, Lau."

"I understand."

"So, how many chances do you give people?" Storm asked, wanting to ensure that her message was embedded in Lauryn's head. She wanted to ensure that Lauryn knew the importance of setting boundaries with people and then holding them accountable when they didn't stick to her boundaries.

"One... and if they cannot respect that then I leave them alone." Lauryn reiterated what her mother had said.

"Good girl," Storm told her as they entered the train station and headed on their way.

AFTER FINDING Lauryn her 'Queen of Hearts' costume that she had been begging for, the two of them made their way to the terminal to explore until it was time for their movie date. Storm's craving for ice cream took over as the two of them approached the corner where Cold Stone sat.

"Do you want ice cream?"

"Yes!" Lau shouted, louder than necessary.

Going inside, they got online to create their ice creams. Once they were done, they found a table in the corner of the establishment and got comfortable.

Twenty-five minutes passed before they had finished their desserts. Getting up out of her seat, Storm pulled her shirt down over her baby bump and back to ensure that none of her skin was exposed. Grabbing the empty cups and used utensils, Storm turned to Lau.

"Come on, lil' girl. We've got an hour before we have to start making our way to the theater and I want to check out a few stores first."

Jumping up from her seat, Lauryn moved with her mother to the garbage and then out of the door while Storm's head was buried in her pocketbook while looking for her phone.

"Oh, excuse me." Storm said after she had bumped into a woman outside of the entrance of Cold Stone. Picking her head up to look at who she had bumped into, Storm was temporarily stuck with surprise. Reaching down, she grabbed ahold of Lauryn's hand and pulled her a little closer to her.

It had been over five years since she'd laid eyes on the woman standing in front of her. Judging from the scowl that was on her face, this interaction was going to be no better than the last inter-action they'd had all those years ago.

"You're excused." The woman sneered, with her eyes on Storm. Storm watched on as the woman's eyes moved from her to Lauryn. For a second, it looked as if tears clouded her vision and her face softened. Just as quickly as Storm thought she had seen that softer side of her, it was replaced with a scowl. Her eyes landed on Storm again before she rolled her eyes and focused on Lauryn again.

"Hi pretty girl," she smiled, before squatting until she was on Lauryn's level.

Tightening the hold that Storm had on Lauryn's hand, she pulled her in closer to her, slightly taking a step-in front of her. "Don't talk to my daughter." Storm growled.

"Well, I thought you wouldn't mind being that you and that no-good bastard that you call a husband are the cause of mine not being here."

"Luciano nor I have shit to do with your daughter not being here… that was all Crystal's crazy ass doing." Came out much faster than Storm had time to process. Once it left her mouth, she wanted to kick herself, but it was too late. She could see the changes it took Crystal's mother, Carol, through.

Instead of responding to Storm, she focused on Lauryn again, "have your parents ever told you about the sister or brother you would have had?"

"Let's go." Storm said, pulling Lauryn with her towards the exit of the mall.

"They probably would have been older than you by a few weeks. My daughter was having a baby with your father." Carol said following behind the two of them, infuriating Storm. This was one of the reasons why she hated not driving... being that the two of them had taken the train, there was no where she could go to get away from the craziness that she had encountered.

"Stop fucking following us!" Storm turned around and screamed, drawing a bit of an audience and scaring Lauryn in the process. Lauryn had never seen her mother react like this and it worried her.

"But your father didn't want the baby he had with my daughter." She said, still following them. The truth was that she was enjoying seeing Storm get riled up, in the past, she tried everything in her power to get a reaction out of Storm and had never been able to. Seeing Storm react today though, was everything she thought it would be for her. Maybe now, Storm would understand how her daughter felt. "He had spent years with my daughter until your mother came along... then when your mother came along, he dropped my daughter with the quickness."

"Baby, don't listen to her." Storm told Lauryn who kept looking back at Carol. Stopping to get Lauryn's attention, "do you hear me?" Storm said to Lauryn. Finally pulling her eyes away from the crazy lady who was following them, Lauryn looked up at her mother with eyes clouded with tears as she shook her head yes.

"Then, your mother wound up pregnant with you when my daughter found out she was pregnant. When she told your father, he told her he wanted a DNA test. Could you believe that?"

Getting back into stride, Storm grabbed her phone out of her bag and went to Erin's number while trying to block out what Carol was saying.

"He wasn't planning on testing you when your mother and

him weren't even together when you were conceived, but he was going to test my grand baby when he knew my child was with him and that she was crazy over him." Carol released a sarcastic laugh.

Storm had her phone to her ear waiting for Erin to answer, counting the rings before she finally got fed up and had to respond. Turning around to face Crystal's mother, Storm said what she had wanted to say for years. "Crazy over him is the perfect description wouldn't you say? So fucking crazy, she killed herself because he didn't want her." Looking to her left, Storm saw that they were being recorded and shook her head. She could kill Carol for the show she was putting on, especially while her child was present. Lauryn was crying hysterically, making Storm's heart ache. There was no way she would be able to fix this without Luck, and she knew it would only be a matter of time before Luck was calling her about it. "For years, y'all have been spewing this same bullshit. Claiming that Luck and I are the cause of your daughter's death. Your daughter was the cause of her own death. We didn't slice her wrist... she did that."

"Storm? Who the fuck are you talking to?" Erin said on the other side of the phone after she answered and heard Storm screaming at someone.

Disregarding Erin, while she still held the phone to her ear, Storm continued. "Luck tried to help her... shit, I even offered to help and talk to her. She refused. That wasn't her first time trying to kill herself either. When Luck tried to end things with her way before I was even a factor, she tried to kill herself then too. What y'all expected him to do? Stay in a relationship where he was unhappy to prevent that crazy ass child of yours from killing herself?" Storm continued, speaking through her anger. By now, Carol was crying hysterically just as Lauryn was, but she had no one to blame but herself. Storm had asked her on more than one occasion to stop following them and leave them alone, but she persisted. Now, she had to deal with the consequences of her actions just like everyone else in the world had to do.

"Where are you, Storm?" Erin was yelling on the other end of the phone with no response from Storm.

"That wasn't his responsibility... hell, had he stayed in that relationship, he probably would have killed himself also. But what you aren't going to do is make our daughter believe that we are the cause of your child or grandchild no longer being here. That was your daughter's fault. She was battling some demons that she should have gotten help for a very long time ago... or at the very least, that y'all should have gotten her help for. Shit, that child she was carrying should have been all the therapy she needed to hold it down, but it wasn't. That was on her, don't blame Lucky or me for her demise. It's not fair!"

Just as the last word left her mouth, Carol lunged at Storm, striking her in her face first before she started swinging wilding, landing hits wherever she could. Screaming, Lauryn released Storm's hand and stepped back from her mother until her back was on the glass of the store they were standing in front of. From there, she watched as the woman continued attacking her mother while Storm did everything in her power to protect her stomach.

After what felt like hours to Storm but was really less than a minute, Carol was pulled off of Storm. A guy was holding Carol back while another guy checked on Storm to make sure she was okay. Full of rage, Storm broke away from the guy that was trying to make sure she was okay, and she rushed to Carol before hitting her with a mean two piece right to the face.

"Damn," could be heard from the spectators as they watched on as blood gushed from Carol's nose.

"You stupid, bitch! You attacked me while my child was holding my hand?" Storm questioned, screaming at the top of her lungs. "While I'm pregnant? Are you stupid?" Storm yelled, raising her hand to hit Carol again but she was stopped by the same guy who had been trying to ensure that she was okay.

"That's enough," he said, moving her away from where Carol was standing.

Looking around for Lauryn, Stormie saw her standing against the Guitar Store's display window crying. "My baby..." Storm exclaimed as she moved to Lauryn. "I'm so sorry. Are you okay?" She asked, dropping to her knees and hugging Lauryn.

After ensuring that Lauryn was okay, Stormie stood up again and grabbed Lau's hand. "Where is my phone?" She questioned, looking around for her phone. The last she remembered, it was in her hand but now, it was nowhere to be found.

"There it is Mommy." Lauryn pulled away from Storm as she ran to get her phone for her.

"Thank you, let's go." Storm grabbed Lauryn's hand again and started once again for the door. The two of them took two steps before the police were walking into the building.

"Shit!" Storm exclaimed. This was the last thing that she needed. She already knew that the video was about to be all over the internet but now that the cops were here, she knew it was going to be bigger than she wanted it to be. Trying to make an exit before the police were alerted that she had been involved in the altercation, she put her head down, grabbed Lauryn's hand a bit tighter, and put a bit of pep in her step.

She was at the door when Carol screamed out, "arrest her, Officers! She attacked me, don't let her leave!" Her outburst caused Storm to stop in her tracks and laugh at the nonsense. Here Carol was screaming for her to be arrested when she was the one who caused all of this mess.

"Ms." One of the officers jogged back over to where Storm was and grabbed a hold of her arm to prevent her from leaving.

Exhaling loudly, Storm turned around and focused her attention on Carol before rolling her eyes and then focusing on the officer.

"It's Mrs. And if you're going to arrest anyone, it needs to be her. She attacked me and endangered the welfare of my children." Storm said, placing her hand on her stomach while looking down at Lauryn.

"Okay, can I get you to step over here for me so that we aren't in the way of the door while I get your statement and we get down to the bottom of this?" The officer asked while pointing to a spot to the right of them.

Doing as she was asked; Storm waited for the officer to get his pad and pen out before she started giving him the rundown of what transpired.

"Sir," one of the guys who had helped to break up the dispute stepped up with another guy beside him. "I'm sorry to interrupt but we were witnesses to what transpired here. I happened to break it up but my pal here was able to record the entire altercation."

"Oh yeah? Can I see it?" The officer asked, giving his undivided attention to the gentleman who had his phone out for the officer to see the video. Pressing play, the four adults watched the video intently as everything played out on his screen.

Fifteen minutes later, the video had finished. Storm asked that the guy send the video to her also. She wanted to ensure that she always had proof to cover her behind should she ever need it. Twenty minutes, a statement and a whole sob story from Carol later, Storm and Lauryn were finally leaving Atlantic Terminal. With her phone ringing off the hook, Storm could bet her last dollar that it was Luck, but she didn't have the mental capacity to answer his call or deal with him at the moment.

Trying to debate on whether she should flag down a cab or

call an Uber, she decided on the latter. Flagging down the first taxi to approach her and Lauryn, they jumped in without a second thought.

After she had given the driver the address to her apartment, she took her phone out and sent a group message to Erin and Amber asking the two of them to meet her at her apartment ASAP. The events of the day had given her an epiphany... one that she had reached a long time ago but had been trying to avoid for just as long.

Putting her phone down once she had sent her message, she turned her attention to Lauryn who was sitting beside her as quiet as a mouse. "I'm so sorry, Lau... for everything that transpired today." Storm said, pulling Lauryn further into her side. "I hate that you had to experience that and even though I wasn't the cause of it getting to that point, I could have done more to ensure that you didn't have to be a witness to that." Hugging Lauryn tightly, Storm started crying. "I'm so sorry, baby." She could only imagine the trauma this day would cause Lauryn. Today was supposed to be a day for Lauryn... a day to take her mind off of everything that was going on between Luck and Storm. Unfortunately, thanks to Carol and her shenanigans, it had gone nothing as planned. Instead of relieving the stress that Lauryn was experiencing, it had added to the stress.

Twenty minutes full of silent cries and hugs, they were finally pulling up to the apartment building that Storm was renting from. Quickly paying the driver and tipping him, Storm woke up a sleeping Lauryn and they made their way up to their apartment.

Walking into their apartment, Storm released a frustrated sigh. She knew today had opened a can of worms and the only thing that she could think of doing to correct it was to call Luck. The two of them needed to have a very long conversation with Lauryn as Storm was sure that she had a lot of questions to ask.

"Go get undressed and comfortable then meet me in the living room so we can talk."

Adhering to her mother's words, Lauryn made her way to her room taking slow strides with her Party City bag in tow.

Taking her own advice, Storm also made her way to her room with her phone in her hand. As soon as she crossed the threshold to her room, her phone began ringing again. Taking a look at the screen, she saw that it was Lucky calling her once again. Closing her door behind her, she answered the phone and placed it on speaker as she began moving around her room.

"Hey," Storm greeted him. The exhaustion from the day could be heard in her voice.

"Are you okay? How's Lauryn?" He asked, sounding just as frantic as she had imagined he would be.

"We're all good. How did you find out?" Storm stupidly asked. She knew how he found out... it took no time for stuff to travel on the internet, especially with the world knowing that she was his wife.

"Instagram... someone sent the video to The Shade Room. Not to mention, Erin called me screaming that something was wrong. Did they take you to the hospital? Where is Lauryn? Let me speak to her." Luck rambled question after question.

"No, I didn't go to the hospital... I'm okay. She didn't hit me in my stomach. And Lauryn is in her room changing. I'll let you speak to her, but you need to come to NY... we need to have a conversation with her together regarding everything that Carol said to her. Besides that, we find out what we're having on Tuesday and I would like you there." Storm said, surprising Luck and herself.

"Alright, I'll look for a flight as soon as I get off of the phone with y'all." Luck said, not wanting to give Storm time to change her mind.

"Okay, well let me get Lauryn for you." Taking the phone off of speaker, Storm threw a t-shirt over her head before heading to

Lauryn's room. Knocking lightly, Storm waited until Lauryn gave her the okay to enter before she pushed open the door to give her the phone.

Seeing the long face Lauryn had made Storm feel horrible. She wished in that moment that she was able to retract the day. "Your daddy is on the phone, Lau." Storm said, handing it to her before turning around to leave out of the room and head back to her room.

Once she was undressed and in her house clothes, Storm headed down to the living room to wait for Lau. As Lauryn finally emerged from her room and down the stairs, there was banging at Storm's door. Stopping mid-step, Lauryn looked at her mom with wide eyes and fear present in her face.

"It's okay, Lau..." Storm told her while getting up from her seat. She was more than a hundred percent sure that it was no one other than Erin and Amber. Her suspicions were confirmed when she peeked out of her peep hole. Opening the door to grant them access to her apartment, Storm waited until they were both inside before closing and locking the door.

"What the hell happened today?!" Amber exclaimed. She was decked out in sweats, a baggy t-shirt and sneakers. Her hair was pulled up in a messy bun with a bandana tied around her edges.

"I don't even know..." Storm answered honestly. She didn't understand how things had gone left so quickly. One minute, Lauryn and her were enjoying their ice cream and the next, Carol was present and acting like a maniac.

"Where the hell is her crazy ass at?"

"I pressed charges. Her ass is at bookings."

"Did you go to the hospital?" Erin asked, looking at Storm's stomach.

"I didn't need to... she never hit me in my stomach." Storm

said, plopping down in her seat next to Lauryn whose attention was in her mother phone while she played a game.

"You still need to go and get checked out, Storm." Erin told her.

"I'm telling you I don't. The baby has been moving ever since I left there. Plus, baby girl's been through enough today. I wanted to come home and talk to her before we had dinner and a movie night."

"So, what you call us over for?" Amber asked.

Inhaling deeply and then slowly releasing it, Storm looked down at Lauryn before focusing her attention back on the girls. "I wanted to let the three of you know that we're going back to LA."

"What?!" Erin, Amber and Lauryn all exclaimed at the same time. Although Amber and Erin wanted her and Luck back together, they didn't wanna lose Storm once again. Even with her always being a phone call away, it wasn't the same as being able to see her in the physical everyday if they wanted to.

"Today was eye opening... had I been in LA, none of this would have happened. Even though I didn't mean for this to happen, I feel like I'm the cause of it." Storm said before she broke down crying, releasing all of the emotions that she had been holding in since everything transpired.

"Storm, no..." Erin said, getting up and running to her side.

"That's bullshit and you know it, Stormie." Amber exclaimed, with tears in her eyes while she stood over Storm. Pulling Storm's head against her stomach, she ran her fingers through Storm's hair to try and comfort her.

"It's not... if I was in Los Angeles, she wouldn't have seen me. She wouldn't have had the chance to traumatize my child... or attack me."

"Storm, you can't blame yourself for the things that other

people do. You were minding your business. This had nothing to do with your decision to stay in New York. Cut it out."

"I agree, but, if you want to go home and work things out with your husband, I completely support that." Amber said, causing Erin to shake her head in agreement.

"You know you don't need an excuse to go home..."

"I know... thank you guys for everything. I know I've been stubborn these past couple of months and living in my feelings. Thank you, guys, for sticking by me even when y'all knew I was dead wrong and strong."

"You don't have to thank us. You stood by us plenty of times we were doing dumb shit. It's only right we return the favor." Amber said, making them all laugh.

"True... but still, thanks."

Standing up, Storm gave the ladies a hug before they got ready to head back to their homes. Walking them to the door, Storm stopped Amber just before she made it out.

"How's your apartment search going, Sis?"

"Horribly. I can't find anything I like in my range. All of these apartments are closets for too much money."

"Well, what about this one?" Storm asked with a smile on her face.

"Which one?" Am asked not quite sure what Storm was trying to say. The place was beautiful, but she couldn't afford to live there. The rent was ridiculous.

"This one... It's paid up for the next year or so... it'll give you time to find something you like without having to deal with that lovely brother of mine."

"Are you serious right now?" Amber asked, excitement starting to course through her veins.

"As a heart attack."

"I love you so much! Thank you so much, Storm!"

"I love you too... when Luck gets here, we can figure everything out as far as you and Autumn moving in here."

"You are the bomb... I swear you are."

"I know... now get out of here so my baby and I can watch some movies and pig out before bed." Storm joked before giving Am and Erin another hug and seeing them out.

Once they were gone, Storm ordered Chinese food and frozen before popping some popcorn and planting herself on the couch with Lauryn for the remainder of the night.

18

"THIS IS YOUR FINAL WARNING... IF YOU TRY THIS SHIT AGAIN, YOU GON' LOSE YOUR WIFE"

-Beyonce'

"*C*an we talk?" Luck was sitting in front of Storm, looking unsure of himself. The two of them had just left the doctor's office after finding out the sex of their baby. Now they were sitting inside of this vegan restaurant that Erin had put Storm onto a few weeks ago named *Greedi Kitchen*. This was the first time that the two of them had seen each other in weeks.

"Talk about what?" Storm asked, even though she was sure that she knew exactly what he wanted to talk about. Storm's suspicions of the little human growing inside of her were confirmed. They were having a little boy and she knew that there was no way Luck would be okay with her and the kids living in New York while he still resided in Los Angeles. Little did he know, she had no plans of staying in New York with the kids anyway.

"About us... we're married, about to have another baby and you're living a whole 2,800 miles away. I can't fly down here for every doctor's visit, Storm. Not to mention your labor. I don't want to miss my son's birth. This shit isn't gonna work... you know that."

"We can make anything work if we put our mind to it, Luciano. You know that better than anyone else in this world of ours." Storm said, not wanting to give in too fast.

"Storm, please. Our kids deserve more than this." The expression that covered Storm's face caused Lucky to keep on talking. "I know that I'm the cause of this divide, but I've been trying for months now to get you to come back home."

"Tryi--" Storm started to cut Lucky off, but he wouldn't allow her to.

"Let me finish, Storm... I've done everything I could think of doing. I've said it so many different ways, but maybe me sitting in front of you and looking you in your face will show you just how serious I am. I want my family back, Stormie. I fucked up; I know that already... I've admitted to that. I thought you had done that fucking surgery and instead of talking to you, I let my pride and ego get in the way. But this has been six months too long, I can't deal with this shit the way it is any longer. I love you and I apologize for everything that I've done to hurt you and cause this split in our union."

Storm's eyes glossed over as she sat there thinking about everything Lucky had said just now.

"How can I fix this, Stormie?" Luck asked, getting up from his seat to move to the other side of the booth where Storm was sitting. Wiping the tears that were cascading down her cheeks, he felt like shit. The last thing he ever wanted was to hurt Storm. Especially causing her any hurt or despair while she was pregnant with his child.

They had prayed for years for the life that she was nesting and it made Luck feel like less than a man that the minute they were blessed with what they had begged God for, they couldn't even enjoy it together.

Even though four and a half months was all that was left of Storm's pregnancy, he was determined to do everything in his power to ensure that she enjoyed the rest of her pregnancy... with him right there with her.

"I don't know, Luciano." Storm answered his question as truthfully as she could. Her response broke not only Lucky's heart, but her own as well. "I wish it was that easy but so much shit has transpired. I don't even know where we start to fix things. I know for a fact that I can never live in that house again. I will never feel the comfort that I used to feel there. Someone else's energy has invaded my home and now resides there... there will never be enough sage in the world to clear it from my home or my head."

Instead of verbally responding to Storm, Luck shook his head up and down to tell her that he had heard her and then he pulled his phone out and sent a text message. Feeling slighted to say the least, Storm's eyes grew into slants as she stared at Lucky in disbelief. Here she was having a very much needed conversation with him and he was texting. Not only did she feel annoyed and disrespected by that gesture, she also felt insecure. It took every-thing in her to not look into his phone to see who he was texting. There was a time when that used to not be her... but it was who she was in that moment.

"Excuse me..." Storm growled while trying to push Luck from the booth so she could get up.

"Where are you going, Storm?" Luck asked, already knowing what the cause of Stormie's change in demeanor was.

"Away from you. Clearly, whatever is in your phone is more important to you than what I'm saying."

"Don't do that, we just spent all of this time apart from each other because we weren't communicating effectively. We got to do better than this... say what's on your mind."

Rolling her eyes, Storm sat there contemplating whether she wanted to speak on the insecurities that were plaguing her or not. Finally saying to hell with it, she decided to speak up. "Who were you texting?"

"Now, was that so hard?" He asked, with a smile on his face. "I was texting the real estate agent. You said you can't live in that house anymore so I'm getting us a new one. What other demands do you have?" Luck asked a quiet Storm.

"Therapy, consistency... I mean, the same things I demanded before we got married. Dedication, love... YOU! If you can't give those things to me, tell me upfront. I can't go through anything like this again, you walking out on me once was it. You pull that shit again, it's over." Storm said with finality. She was sporting her best poker face, but she knew that she wouldn't be any good if it really was the end of their relationship.

"You got it." Luck said with no hesitation at all.

"Are you sure? Don't write a check..."

"What do you mean am I sure? Why wouldn't I be sure?"

"I mean, the last time I needed you, you ran. The last few times I've needed you actually, you ran. On top of that, you didn't just run from me, you ran from Lau also for a while simply to stay away from me. I can't take that again... *we* can't take it again. It's either you're here or you're not. Either you're sure you can be here and consistent or we have to call it quits." Storm said with finality.

"Even though at the moment, I know my word probably

doesn't mean shit to you, I promise that you have my word. I'll never not be there when you need me again. You can put your life on that."

Staring him in the eyes, Storm tried to get the truth from his soul. His soul was telling her that he meant what he said, but still she was hesitant. *Am I doing the right thing?* Kept running through her mind repeatedly while she sat there staring at Luck.

Sensing her hesitation, Luck grabbed her hand and ran his thumb along the top of her hand before scooting a little bit closer to her. "You with me, Storm?"

Thinking for a few more minutes, Storm shook her head yeah with tears brimming in her eyes. "But this is the last time. If you let me down again..." Storm started but Luck kissing her cut her short.

"I promise," Luck said before leaning in to kiss Storm again. "I promise," he reiterated once their kiss had finished.

"Can you trust that?" Luck asked Storm. When she put her head down instead of responding to him, he placed a finger under her chin prompting her to look at him.

"Storm..."

"If I don't trust anything else, I trust our love... I trust love." Storm started. "Despite everything that we've gone through over these past couple of months, I still love you. As much as I have hated you in these past few months, I've loved you just as much. As much as I didn't want to be anywhere near you, I couldn't resist the pull you had on me. So yes, I can trust that, but I promise you this is it. If we can't get it right this time, that's it."

With a smile a mile long, Luck rejoiced internally. He felt accomplished. He had thought about this moment for months and even though it wasn't exactly the way he had planned it out, it still turned out the same... he got his wife and kids back and he would forever be thankful for that. Although Storm was still unsure of his word, he knew that she had no reason to be. He knew what life was like without her, he made a promise to himself that he would never experience that again.

"Thank you, God." He muttered before the waiter approached the table to take their orders.

19

"I WAS ON A ROLL, YOU ANOTHER WIN."

Nipsey Hussle

"How much longer do you think it'll take before we find a new house?" Storm asked Luck. They were sitting in the living room of the apartment Storm had been renting while living in New York. The five of them, Amber and Autumn included, had been living there for the past month and a half.

Staying true to her word, Storm refused to go back to Los Angeles if they were going to be living in the home Luck had infiltrated with the presence of another woman.

Luck refused to go back to Los Angeles without Storm and Lauryn, therefore making New York his permanent residence, temporarily. He had already missed so much time with the two of them and there was no way he would miss anymore, especially with his baby boy still growing inside of Lauryn. He didn't want to miss anything.

However, with about three months left of her pregnancy and still not being able to find a house, Storm was growing frantic. Soon, she wouldn't be permitted to travel and on top of that, there was no way that she would be able to move and situate a new house with a huge belly preceding her. She wanted to have everything prepared for the baby when he was brought home, she already knew how hectic it would be with a new baby and Lauryn, she didn't want to add any other stress.

"I'm not sure, Storm all I know right now is that the real estate agent is doing the best they can. With the demands you've requested it is almost impossible for us to find a place. That's why I had the last house built, we don't have that kind of time this time around, though." Luck was frustrated with this process as well.

Although Storm's apartment was nice, it was way too small for the five of them... soon to be six. Not to mention, Luck was over New York. It was starting to get cold and he was remembering all too well why he jumped at the opportunity to move to Los Angeles all those years ago.

"You say that like my request were outlandish. I only requested that we have an enclosed patio, a multiple car garage, five bedrooms, three bathrooms, a lot of closet space, carpet, a basement, backyard and lots of windows among a few other things." Storm was staring at Luck incredulously like what she had asked for was not a lot while Luck was looking at her like she had multiple heads.

"Storm, you're asking for the world in a short amount of time. I hope you aren't planning on making it back to Los Aneles before the baby is born because that's not going to happen." Luck was frustrated and it could be heard vividly in his tone.

Storm wanted to bring up the fact that their house would have still been operable had Luck not infiltrated it with another woman. She kept those thoughts and words at bay though. *All is forgiven, you can't throw that back in his face, Storm.*

"That's because you are saying stuff like that. You do know that the universe hears you when you make little declarations like that, right? We will find a place and be moved in before our son gets here. The agent is just not looking in the right places." Storm stated matter of factly. Pulling her phone out, she went to the Zillow app to do some more searching herself. For the past couple of weeks, she'd been on Zillow like it was Instagram and she had no complaints.

If it meant getting back to Los Angeles, then she was going to exhaust every option there was. Although she loved being in New York and being close to family, especially while she was pregnant, she had to admit that the weather was something that she also wasn't used to.

Fall had come and just about gone. Where there were 70 and 60-degree days in Los Angeles, they were experiencing 40 and 30-degree days in New York. Storm or Lauryn hadn't owned a winter coat in years, and they hadn't planned on making this year any different, but they had no choice.

"How about we check out some places next week... I have to go to LA for a few meetings and shows and I need you there with me. I haven't had an assistant or manager in half a year damn near. It's time for you to get back to work."

The past month and a half, Luck had taken time off from work, canceling all appearances, shows, hostings and meetings. He wanted to focus on his family, pampering his wife and daughter and getting him and Storm back to where they needed to be. He had done that tirelessly and now; it was time to return to work.

"I'm going to go with you to Los Angeles for a week and who will keep our daughter?" Storm asked, knowing that it was a stupid question. Both of their families were in New York, there were a plethora of people capable and more than willing to hold Lauryn down for them while they were away on business. The truth was that Storm wasn't sure that she wanted to return to work just yet.

She had been gone for months now and she knew that a host of people had pieced together the on goings of their relationship. Although Storm didn't necessarily care what people thought about her or said about her, with her being pregnant, she was more sensitive and looking to protect her feelings.

"Seriously, Storm? Are you worrying about what people will say because you haven't been around for a while and now, you're back?" Luck asked, hitting the nail on the head.

Unwillingly, Storm shook her head as tears welled in her eyes. "Why the fuck am I crying?" Storm belted out, frustrated with the up and down of her emotions lately.

Blowing out an exasperated breath, Storm wiped her face free from the eyes and got herself together mentally before she responded to Luck's question.

"Yeah, for some stupid ass reason, I am worrying about what people will think or say... not that it matters. That ain't even me.

"It's not you, but even if it was, understand that all that matters is us. We're happy, fuck what people think or say. Shit, their situations are probably worse than ours ever could be." Luck told Storm walking over to her.

"You're right. I don't know what's wrong with me." Allowing Luck to help her up from where she was sitting, Storm wrapped her arms around his waist and hugged him. "Thank you for bringing me back."

"You don't have to thank me for that, babe. That's what I'm here for." Hugging Storm back, he leaned down and gave her a kiss to her forehead first and then a kiss to her nose before kissing her lips.

Storm, always in the mood to have sex lately, deepened the kiss.

"Umm," Luck moaned before pulling away.

"Whyyy?" Storm whined with a pout gracing her beautiful face almost simultaneously.

"We have moves to make, baby."

Rolling her eyes, Storm stomped off from Luck to make her way to the back of the apartment so she could start getting dressed.

"Stop being so spoiled," Luck chuckled, following behind her. "I just broke you off three times not even two hours ago. I got you when we get back but right now, we gotta go and get our outfits, my hair cut and get your hair and nails done for the maternity pictures that you cried about taking." Luck reminded Storm as he stood in the doorway watching her throw on sweatpants and one of his hoodies.

"Whatever... let's go." Storm fussed with him the second she had the clothes pulled on.

"You aren't going to do anything to your hair?" Luck asked, regretting it the minute the words were out of his mouth.

"My hair is fine as it is." Storm said, giving Luck evil eyes. Her hair was standing all over her head... she was rocking an old twist out that she had slept on for the past three days. Her hair was in dire need of water and oil, but Storm was so frustrated that she didn't give a damn.

"You can be mad all you want, but your ass is going to do something to that head before we walk out of here." Luck told her, meaning every word he said.

Stubbornly standing there, Storm stared at Lucky with a stone face before she burst out laughing. "You foul as fuck for that. You're supposed to love me regardless of how I look."

"Yeah, I do... when we're in the house. But when it's time to hit the streets..." Luck laughed. "You know paparazzi don't waste no time. You might want to handle that."

"Ugh, give me another ten minutes. I'm just going to put this shit in a pineapple."

"My favorite style." Luck reminded her as he made his way back to the living room to wait for Storm.

Roughly ten minutes later, Storm was back in the living room with her hair put up in a 'fineapple', as Luck always called it. She had spent some extra time on her baby hairs to help bring the style together, and Luck was appreciative.

Storm's face had gained a lot of weight... something she wasn't happy about but something Luck loved about her. Overall, Storm had gained about twenty pounds, most of its baby but some of it had filled in her thighs and her ass. Whereas a lot of women lost their butt when they were pregnant, Storm had gained a bigger one.

Luck loved everything about her pregnancy this time. When she was pregnant with Lauryn, her body didn't have all of these changes. He was thankful that he hadn't missed her entire pregnancy. He was already kicking himself in the butt for missing damn near half of it but had he missed the entire thing... he would have hated himself.

"Let's roll." Standing up and grabbing his keys and cell phone from the coffee table, before grabbing Stormie's hand and leading her out of the house.

"I'M EXHAUSTED... we should have done everything over the course of a week instead of the day before. I'm gonna look horrible tomorrow with bags and shit under my eyes." Storm complained as Luck and her finally made it back to the house. It wouldn't have been so bad had it not been a Friday. The mall was packed, the hair salon was packed, along with the barbershop and the nail salon.

Storm and Luck thought they would be done in time to get Lauryn from school, but here it was after 10 o'clock and they were just getting back home from 11 a.m. this morning.

"Yeah, I didn't expect to be out all day like that either." Luck admitted as well. He planned on getting everything needed and getting his hair cut before picking Storm up and playing the house for the rest of the day.

Walking into the house with an unreasonable number of bags for their maternity photos, Luck placed them down at the entry way of the living room before he stepped out of his shoes and plopped down on the couch next to Storm.

"Lau!" Storm yelled for Lauryn. It had been a long day and she wanted nothing more than to go to sleep right then and there but she also missed her baby girl. It was rare that Storm wasn't there to pick Lau up. Their mother daughter time together was sacred to them both. Whenever they couldn't get their quality time in, Storm made it her business to make up for it.

"Lauryn!" Storm shouted again when she got no response. It was already a little after 10:40 p.m. and normally, Lauryn would be asleep but with it being the weekend and no school tomorrow, she wasn't so sure.

"Stop calling her, she's asleep." Amber said, walking from the back of the house dressed in a pair of grey sweats and a black t-shirt. She was shoeless, no sneakers, no socks, no slippers.

"I'm just making sure..."

"Y'all got everything y'all needed for tomorrow?"

"If we didn't, we don't need it." Luck said, plopping down on the couch. He was beat, he would never understand how women could shop all day and still not be tired in the end.

"You're right about that." Storm co-signed, picking her feet up from the ground to place in Luck's lap. Her feet were swollen almost double their normal size.

"Damn Storm, why your feet and ankles swollen like that?" Amber asked rushing over to where Storm and Luck were sitting on the sofa to further inspect her feet.

"I been on them all day walking around." Storm said looking down at her feet with Luck and Amber.

"Nah, this is more than you just being on them all day, Storm. You feel okay?" Amber asked worried. There was no way Storm's feet, ankles and legs should have been as big as they were.

"Yeah, I feel fine. Stop fussing. I just been on my feet all day... shit, damn near twelve hours." Removing her feet from Luck's lap and struggling to stand up.

"I don't know, Storm. Amber's right... your feet don't look good."

Rolling her eyes, Storm started up the stairs. "I'm okay guys. For real, I'm going to take a shower and lay down, I'm okay."

20

"I REPRESENT AN ENTIRE GENERATION..."

-Nicki Minaj

"*B*aby, wake up."

It was after three in the morning and Storm had been woken up with horrible pains. Thinking she needed to go to the bathroom, she had gone and sat on the toilet only for her water to break.

"Baby... you gotta wake up." Storm said, shaking him a little harder.

"What? What's wrong?" Luck asked halfway in consciousness and halfway out.

"My water broke." Storm said, scaring Luck. He jumped up in the bed and stared at her until her words had sunken in.

"What do you mean your water broke?"

"It just broke."

"Okay, don't panic." Luck was one to talk. He was panicking

already as he jumped out of bed and started stepping into clothes without taking off his pajamas. Storm was only six months, there was no reason that her water should have broken. She still needed to nest for the next three months. "Get some clothes on Storm." Luck demanded.

"I'm already dressed." Luck hadn't even been paying attention to Storm but now that he looked, he saw that she was dressed. Her face was contorted in pain and her breathing labored.

"Shit, we haven't even packed a bag yet. We aren't ready for this." Luck fussed as he moved around the room in circles trying to get himself and Storm together.

"Don't worry about that. We have to get to the hospital now, it's too soon for me to be in labor. If we need anything else, you can come back and get it." Storm was already moving towards the door of their bedroom.

"Alright." Luck was right behind her after grabbing his wallet and keys.

While in route to the front door, Storm knocked on Amber's door before walking in.

"Am, Am... get up."

"What's the matter?"

"My water broke, we're going to the hospital."

Jumping out of bed the same way that Luck had jumped out, Amber was on her feet and at Storm's side inspecting her in no time.

"Your water broke? It's too soon..."

"That's why we're heading out of here now. Send Lauryn to school in the morning then come to the hospital afterwards, okay?" Storm asked even though she knew that Amber would take care of everything.

"Call me once you know something." Amber was nervous for Storm. She had already experienced giving birth to a still born and it had been hell on Storm. Hell, it had been hell on the family, but it had just about broken Storm. She wasn't herself for a year afterward and Amber knew Storm couldn't withstand anything like that again. Silently, she prayed that everything would work itself out. She prayed that God would cover Storm and the baby.

Once Amber had seen Storm and Luck off, she started making phone calls to alert everyone of what was going on.

THE FETAL MONITOR that Storm was hooked up to revealed that her contractions were about 15 minutes apart. The cervix examination also uncovered that she was two centimeters dilated. The minute the doctors had realized that she was really in labor at 26 weeks, they began doing everything they could to stop her labor.

She'd been admitted to the hospital and the doctors had started an IV on her and magnesium sulfate to stop the contractions that she was experiencing. The cervical examination also proved that there was no infection.

Her doctor had been in first thing this morning to see her. After giving her an ultrasound, the doctor found that there was still some fluid around the baby. She told Storm that if the medicine worked and her labor was able to be stopped, they would let her go home after 48 hours but Storm would be on bedrest for the remainder of her pregnancy and her appointments would be two times a week instead of once a month. Storm was fine with all of that as long as she was able to bring a healthy baby boy into the world, she'd do whatever she needed to do.

"I knew something wasn't right, especially the other day when we were doing that damn maternity shoot. You could barely stand up. Your feet were swollen double the size, you were having back pains and all those complaints of gas... it was probably contractions thinking about it now." Luck fussed with Storm. He had been trying to get Storm to go to the doctor for the past three days, but Storm was bullheaded. She refused to go to the hospital, her excuse was that she had a doctor's visit at the end of this week, she claimed she would be fine until then. Clearly, that was a lie.

"I thought it was gas. They weren't pains that I couldn't deal with." Storm argued her point.

"How long were you feeling like that? The maternity shoot was two days ago, Storm."

"Since the day before the shoot when we went shopping. I thought I had gas all this time."

"Next time be safe rather than sorry. This could have had a different ending, Storm." Pam said. She had been worried out of her mind all morning. As soon as Amber called her this morning, she said a prayer for Storm and then she went to get Adelasia. The two of them had made it to the hospital thirty minutes after Lucky and Storm made it there and had been there all morning with the two of them.

"I agree, Storm. If you even sneeze wrong, you need to be going to the doctor." Amber said. Her nerves were shot, she had been so worried, she couldn't get the kids off to school fast enough this morning.

"Alright, y'all not about to gang up on my sister." Steven said, speaking up for Storm. He could see the effect their words were having on her. Although he did agree with them, he would tell Storm that at a later time. Right now, wasn't the time. "Thankfully, everything is fine. We aren't going to dwell on the 'what could be.'" Leaning over to Storm, Steven gave her kiss on her forehead before whispering to her that he loved her.

"You're right, Steven, this was a learning experience for all of us." Erin said, sensing the change in Storm's attitude, as well. To Erin, it felt like everyone was ganging up on Storm, she could only imagine what Storm was feeling, especially with her hormones all out of whack.

"Nah, they're right... I should have known something was wrong. Especially with all of the complications I've experienced. How stupid could I have been?" Storm said, being just as hard on herself as everyone else was being.

"Storm, no." Adelasia said, moving from her seat to where Storm was laying in the hospital bed. "You didn't know. That's not stupid. No one ever thinks the worse when things are going on with them. Hell, I would have disregarded it too thinking it was gas. Thank God everything is okay with you and mio nipote, that's all that matters."

Silence followed as everyone processed what Adelasia said, shaking their heads as everyone realized that she was right. They were all guilty of disregarding the signs their body gave them when something was wrong. Always thinking it was something less serious. Hell, Erin ignored her body for damn near four months when she was pregnant with Damia.

The door opening of Storm's hospital room pulled everyone from their own personal thoughts. "Hi family." Storm's GYN, Dr. Smith, said as she walked to the wall that housed the gloves. "Can I ask you guys to step out for a few so that I can check on Mommy and baby boy?"

"Sure. We'll be in the waiting room." Pam informed Storm and Luck after she had finished gathering her belongings.

"You hungry, Sis?" Amber asked as she too gathered her belongings.

"Starving. Is there a Chick-Fil-A around here?" Storm asked even though she knew that there wasn't.

"You know there isn't, but I'll find one for you... I already know what you want." Heading to the door, Amber was just about out when Steven jumped up and said he was going with her.

"No, the hell you aren't." Amber blurted before letting the door close behind her causing everyone left in the room to laugh at her.

For the last few weeks, Steven had been chasing behind Amber something seriously and she had been dodging all of his advances.

Steven was shocked when Amber moved out with Autumn. Even though he knew that he had been slipping and getting sloppy with the shit he was doing, he wasn't expecting her to make a move like that.

"These two," Erin said, shaking her head as she followed out of the door behind them. "Storm, we'll be back."

Once the door was closed after they had all left, the doctor went on to check Storm.

"THE NEXT THREE and a half months are going to be hell." Storm commented the moment they had pulled up to their apartment building.

Storm had just been released from the hospital a little over an hour ago. Having spent the last two days in the hospital, she was dying for some fresh air and good food. For the past few days, she had been craving Juniors French Toast, strawberry cheesecake and her window seat so she could people watch while she enjoyed Luck's company. Luck wasn't with it though. He was taking the doctors' orders seriously. Instead, he made Storm wait in the car while he went into Juniors and ordered their food. Afterwards, he drove the two of them home.

Storm was pissed but what could she do? They were currently getting out of the car and making their way to the building;

Storm with a bad attitude and Luck feeling exactly what Storm had just said.

"Tell me about it. You're about to be a brat."

"Fuck you. I'm not a brat but when they said bed rest, I don't think that meant that I couldn't go sit at a restaurant and eat."

"That's exactly what it meant, Storm. Bed rest means bed rest. What difference does it make if you eat it there or if you eat it at home?"

"I wanted to people watch and enjoy the hustle and bustle of the busy life." Storm whined.

"Turn on the television. What's better than lunch in bed? You can relax and get straight to a nap."

Instead of responding, Storm rolled her eyes and followed behind him with a pout in her face. The back and forth wouldn't help a thing now. They were already home.

After undressing and getting comfortable, Storm was in the bed with her to go plate, the remote, and a gallon of water. Even though she would have preferred to stay at the restaurant, she had to admit that the beds comfortability was on everything.

"What are you doing?" Storm asked Luck when she saw that he too was getting undressed.

"Getting in the bed with you." Luck said, climbing in the bed beside her.

"Well, I can clearly see that, but why? I thought you had running around to do."

"I did, but it can wait. Right now, I want to make sure you don't bore yourself to death."

"You don't have to do that, boo." Although Storm loved the idea of spending all day in bed with Luck, she knew there were things that needed Luck's attention.

"I know I don't *have* to but I'm going to, unless you don't want me to." Luck gave Storm a questioning glare midway to him getting in the bed beside her while he waited for her to respond.

"Boy, get your ass in this bed." Storm said, stuffing her mouth with her first bite of French toast.

"That's what I thought." Luck said, plopping down on the bed, almost causing Storm to drop her food in the process.

"You better be glad my food didn't fall, motherfucker. Otherwise, your ass would have been going back to Junior's to get me another order of this."

"Yeah the fuck right. I wasn't getting nothing." Luck joked but he knew that if Storm asked him, he was going to get it for her, no questions asked.

"Oh yeah?" raised eyebrows and a surprised look covered her face.

"I'm just playing, I'm just playing."

"... GOT THE HAMMER AND THE WRENCH"

-Nicki Minaj

"*Yo sis, what's up?*" Steven asked as soon as Storm answered her phone.

"*Shit... I'm tired of being in the bed all day every day but little man has my body until he makes it here.*" Storm fussed, voicing her frustrations. She had been in the bed for the last month and it was driving her crazy.

Her Christmas and New Year had both been spent in the bed and although everyone had tried their best to make it memorable and enjoyable—Luck especially, it hadn't worked.

Storm was now 36 weeks pregnant and still two centimeters dilated. Although her doctor said she was in the safe zone now if she went into active labor again, Storm was not trying to hear it. She wanted to go her full 40 weeks to ensure that there were no complications with her baby boy when he finally made his arrival into this world.

"Well, I'm coming to get in bed with you today. I have food with me and your favorite movies." Steven said. He was already in route to her. Thanks to her being bed ridden, he knew that she wasn't anywhere but in the house.

"Oh yeah? And to what do I owe the pleasure of this visit?"

"What do you mean? I can't come and visit my sister?" Feigning ignorance wasn't his best choice because he knew Storm had no problem putting anyone on their ass when they tried to play on her intelligence.

"You could if that's all this was but I've been in New York since the summer... it's the end of January now and I can count on one hand how many times I've seen you and spent time with you."

"I was working heavy during the summer... I got time now."

"Bullshit, as busy as your dick was this summer?" Storm started to go in.

"Man, Amber got you believing that shit too, huh?"

"We'll talk when you get here because this is a conversation I've been dying to have." Instead of waiting for Steven's response, Storm hung up on him.

Twenty minutes later, Storm's doorbell was ringing. Getting up from the bed, she took her time making it to the door.

"I thought your ass fell asleep or something, it took you that long to walk to the door?" Steven complained after giving Storm a hug and a kiss.

"Oh, you got jokes?" Storm laughed. *"Just be happy I opened the door for your lying ass."*

"Here we go. Why I gotta be all of that?"

"Because you are and what's blowing my mind is why you're lying. Especially to me... we never did that." Storm said, climbing back in

bed after she had made it back to her room with the assistance of Steven.

Steven remained quiet while he took off his coat and shoes before going to the bathroom to change into the pajama pants that he had brought with him from home. He knew how anal Storm could be when it came to people sitting on her bed with their outside clothes. She had been that way since a child and although back then it had driven him mad, now, he understood why.

Walking back into the room after he had changed, Steven said what he had been debating on admitting. "You're right... I fucked up."

"I already knew you did."

"No, you all were assuming." Handing Storm the French toast and sausage that he had gotten for her from Juniors.

"Do you really believe that?" With the fork stopping midway to her mouth, Storm looked at Steven with questioning eyes. "Let me put you on to something."

Putting her fork and her to-go plate down on the bed beside her, Storm gave Steven her undivided attention.

"As a woman, you don't need proof. Proof is that feeling in your gut that something isn't right. It's that feeling that something is going on behind your back that you aren't aware of. It's when your man comes home and instead of hugging and kissing on you like he normally does; he's washing up in the bathroom. It's when you call your man and his phone is going to the voice-mail or he isn't answering like he normally does. We don't need proof. We have spidey senses that alert us the minute our man looks at a woman too long." Storm told Steven.

"Get the fuck out of here, Storm. That isn't proof." Cracking up laughing, Steven couldn't believe that Storm was calling intuition facts. "If you don't see it with your own eyes or hear it with your own ears then it's not fact."

"Well, what do you call seeing a video of your husband in a club fucking a woman that isn't you?" Storm blurted out before picking her food back up and eating a fork full of French toast.

"What?" Choking on the food he had been chewing up, he was sure that he had heard her wrong. There was no way anyone had seen him doing anything of the sort... Steven waited for Storm to tell him she was lying while his heart danced in the pit of his stomach.

"You heard me. We watched the video... all three of us."

"Why the fuck wouldn't Amber tell me that?"

"What difference would it have made? You had already fucked the woman and Amber had already made her mind up. That would have been a pointless conversation."

"It would have made a hell of a difference. I could have worked this shit out with my wife, Storm. Why didn't you or Erin tell me what was going on?!" By now, Steven was yelling. He now understood why this split up with Amber felt so different... it was.

"First of all, don't yell at me. This didn't have shit to do with Erin or I. Shit, I said too much already because you were never supposed to know that Amber knew about that damn video. Either way, this was your fuck up. You have no one to blame but yourself. Especially since I told your ass in advance that this is where you were headed. You chose to continue on with your BS instead of making shit work with your wife, for your daughter, nigga." Storm said, just as excited as Steven was. With the last word she spoke, a pain shot from her lower back through her stomach causing her to drop her plate of food and clutch her stomach.

"What's wrong?" Steven asked, forgetting all about the

conversation they were having only seconds ago. Seeing Storm in distress gave him memory loss.

"I— argh!" Storm screamed again, buckling over on the bed.

"I'm calling an ambulance." Steven said aloud, grabbing his phone and dialing 911 without a second thought.

"I have to take a shit." Storm blurted out while throwing the covers off of her body and attempting to get out of the bed while Steven explained everything to the operator.

"The operator said no!" He shouted back at her while making his way to her.

"What does she mean no? I have to go."

"That's the baby." Steven said, listening intently to what the operator was saying.

"Lay down, Storm."

"For what? I just said I have to use the toilet."

"No, you need to push my nephew out. Lay down... I have to check you."

"What?!"

"Just do it!"

Laying back down on the bed, Storm pulled her pajama pants and underwear off. She felt uncomfortable as fuck as Steven looked between her legs.

"I need to push." Storm whined, the urge becoming more prevalent now than before.

"I see his head." Steven shouted, fear plaguing him as he thought about what he was really about to do.

Putting the phone on speaker and laying it on the bed next to him and Storm, Steven followed the instructions of the operator. Thirty minutes later, Storm, Steven and baby Sage were in the back of an ambulance making their way to the hospital.

. . .

"Shit, you are delivering babies and shit now, nigga?" Luck said with a smile on his face.

He had arrived at the hospital forty minutes ago and had rushed to see Storm and his son. He was kicking himself in the ass because something had told him that he should stay home today but he wanted to hit the studio for a few hours and get some songs knocked out while they were fresh on his mind. Those few songs cost him his son's birth though.

"Man, thank God I am delivering them otherwise my nephew would have been born in the toilet." Steven joked.

"Nah, for real though, thank you. I know that's your sister but that's my heart. Thank you for being there and making sure she got my son here safely."

"You know better, that's my heart too... I'm gonna have her regardless but I hear what you're saying, and I respect it so you got it, bro."

"Love." Luck said as he reached his hand out to give his brother in law a pound.

"Love." Steven repeated.

"How much longer do you two have plans on staying in NY with the kids?" Steven asked. The two were waiting in the hallway while the doctors checked on Storm and Sage.

"Maybe another few weeks. The realtor finally found something that fits all of the requirements Storm gave her." Luck laughed, shaking his head.

"You know she's going to go over and above to make you pay for ruining her humble abode." Steven said, knowing Storm all too well.

"Yeah, I know. I don't even care though if I'm being honest. As long as my wife is home with my kids, that's all that matters."

"Shit, I hear you on that. I'm trying to figure out how to get my wife home now." Steven admitted.

"Good luck with that... I been hearing the conversations, man."

"Aw, man. Don't say that shit."

"I'm just being honest, bro. I don't know how you're gonna pull yourself out of that shit."

"I don't know either but I'm going to figure it the fuck out. Life hasn't been the same since her and Autumn left."

"I'll see what I can do on my end but good luck, nigga." With his last words came the rest of the family. All pouring in with big smiles, all excited to have a new little one.

22

"WHEN LOVING YOU STARTS TO HURT ME, I HAVE TO STEP OFF... & I'M SORRY IF THAT HURTS YOU."

-Sky EM

"So, how does it feel being new parents again after five years?" Amber asked the morning after Storm and Sage had made it home from the hospital.

"Like I haven't slept in a month of Friday's. I forgot that this was what life was like with a newborn."

"I know. That little boy has some lungs on him. I listened to his ass scream all night. Shit, I don't know how the girls got any sleep last night.

"Don't do my boy, Am. We fam and all but you still aren't no match for Sage." Luck spoke finally.

"That's okay, Storm has my back."

"Nah, sis. Luck is right on this one. I'm going to jail or hell behind mine."

"Damn, that's how you do me after I've listened to you cry,

moan and groan with your stubborn, indecisive behind? I bet I won't do that again." Amber joked as she cleaned up her dishes from the breakfast she'd made after dropping Lauryn and Autumn off to school earlier that morning.

"That's what your mouth says now but the second I need you; you'll be there. You always are." Storm admitted.

"At least you know."

"Yo sis, you still ain't fucking with Steven?" Lucky asked completely from left field.

"You know she ain't fucking with him, why would you ask her that?" Storm answered for Amber, taking offense to his question as if she herself were Amber.

"Damn, Amber!" Lucky replied, looking at Storm incredulously.

"She said what I was thinking." Amber spoke up followed by a shrug of her shoulders.

"He misses you... he—"

"Get the fuck out of here." Amber blurted, cutting Lucky and his attempt at advocating for Steven off. "He doesn't miss me, that's bullshit. He misses having someone around to do all the shit he's too lazy to do." Laughing, Amber shook her head before continuing. "How could he miss me? When I was there, he paid me no attention. Shit, he's the cause of me living somewhere other than the place that's been my home for damn near ten years. Yet, he misses me... yeah, he needs to miss me with that shit." Amber was flabbergasted. How dare Steven... how dare Luck for even repeating the bullshit Steven had slewed to him.

"I'm just saying, sis... when we spoke a few days ago, it sounded like he realized he made a mistake and he wanted to make it right."

"Again, I'm calling bullshit. Children make mistakes, adults make decisions. He knew what he was doing, he knew what he was risking. What he didn't know was how I was going to react. His ass made his bed, now he has to lie in it."

"So, you really don't see any resolution to this?" Luck had to ask to be sure.

"Absolutely, it'll be resolved when we get a divorce."

"A *divorce*?!" Luck shouted, shocked that Amber had taken it that far. Yeah, he knew what had been going on lately between the two of them, but he also knew the history between the two of them. They had been through this and gotten through this many times before, he thought that this time would be similar to all of the other times.

"That sounds about right... I've loved that man for years and the more I love him, the more it hurts me. Where is the love in that?"

"Damn," looking to Storm, Luck's eyes held a sadness for the state of Steven and Amber's relationship. Things were bad between them, but he didn't know they were that bad.

"Anyway, what's the word on the new house?" Amber asked changing subjects quickly while taking Sage out of his rocker the moment he started fussing to hand to Storm for his feeding.

Although Amber claimed that she was good with just Autumn, she secretly wanted more children... however, it looked like that would be going out of the window along with her husband.

"It's ready. We're just going to wait until Storm and Sage have their six-week checkups. Then, we're out of here." Lucky informed her. He was glad that they would be heading back home soon. He loved New York, it would always be home, but he couldn't wait to be back in Los Angeles. That was his home now and he loved it.

"I was hoping you were going to say that they were still having a hard time finding a place for you guys. I don't want y'all to leave." Amber admitted, feeling vulnerable. The breakup with her and Steven was easy right now because she had Storm there to feed off of her energy and keep her company but the minute Storm left, she knew it was going to hit her and hit her hard.

"I mean, you could always come with us..." Storm playfully suggested but little did she know, she had just put an idea in Ambers mind that would live and fester for the next few weeks.

"THIS IS BITTERSWEET." Storm said as she packed the last of her and Lucks belongings for their return back to Los Angeles.

Her 6-week checkup had come and gone last week and finally, they were ready to head back. Tomorrow, they'd be shipping their belongings off before the family of four boarded the plane from JFK to LAX tomorrow night.

"I know. It was bittersweet all those years ago too." Luck reminded her.

"I remember. When we first moved to LA, I cried for damn near a month." Storm reflected. Although she was happy for the opportunities that were afforded to her and Luck at the time, she still missed her family.

"Yeah, I thought I was going to have to ship your crying ass back here." Luck chuckled as he thought back on when they first relocated.

"Oh, please! You weren't shipping me back nowhere. You would have missed me too much."

"Yeah, you're right. I would have missed you a lot, but I would have been alright, eventually."

"Oh yeah?" Storm asked, attitude on the brinks.

"Nah, I would have come back with you... we would have been bi-coastal until you were ready to make the move officially." Luck said, telling the truth.

"Good answer!" Storm laughed, brightening up immediately.

"We better get up and start getting ready for dinner tonight. Plus, you know your cry baby son is going to be up soon wailing for some breast milk."

In six weeks, Sage had shaken everything around him up. Everyone in the house moved on his time. They ate when he gave them time, changed him when he wanted to be changed, picked him up when he wanted to be picked up and ate as soon as his stomach growled. He was demanding and gave no fucks who had to wait until he got what he wanted.

"Yeah, I know his little bossy self will be. Let me jump in the shower now. Babe, can you pack him a bag please?" Storm asked as she grabbed her towel already in route to the bathroom.

"I got you."

Thirty minutes later, Storm was sitting on the side of the bed with a towel wrapped around her as she rubbed shea butter on her feet and legs.

A knock on her bedroom door prompted her to tell who she knew was Lauryn to come in.

"Look at how pretty you look." Storm told Lau as soon as she stepped through her door. Dressed in a light pink, tan and brown long-sleeved patchwork dress with matching patchwork UGGs, the colors really complimented Lauryn. Yesterday, Storm had braided her hair into a Mohawk and put little jewels in her hair as well.

"Thank you, mommy." Lauryn said, her attention on Sage and Sage only.

"Don't wake him, I have to finish getting myself together first."

"I won't. I'll watch him until you finish." Lauryn said, sitting on the side of the bed where Sage's bassinet was strategically placed.

Grabbing the remote from the nightstand, Storm turned on the television and turned to cartoons before adjusting the volume for Lauryn so that she would be able to hear it and it wouldn't wake Sage up in the same breath. Once that was done, Storm got up from the bed and made her way to the almost empty closet to choose what she would wear from the few outfits she had left out for tonight's dinner with the family. Everyone wanted to see them off before they returned back to Los Angeles.

Deciding on a pair of vintage green high waisted pants with suspenders and a white top that tied into a bow at the neck, Storm felt excited. It had been over a month since she had gotten dressed up, her life had revolved around Sage for the past month and a half. She wasn't complaining a bit, but she missed feeling like herself.

After she had gotten dressed, Storm grabbed a pair of yellow chunky heels to match her outfit. Walking back into the bedroom, Storm smiled at Lauryn who was fully engrossed in her cartoons. Sitting at the vanity table that was placed in the corner of the room, Storm turned on the lights and applied light makeup before taking out her twist.

The second she had finished; Lucky was walking into the room with his boxers on and his towel draped around his neck.

"Damn!" He exclaimed. Storm looked gorgeous. She had given birth only a month and a half ago, but you couldn't tell if you didn't know. Thanks to breast feeding, she had dropped damn near all of her baby weight. Storm was ecstatic about that, but Luck loved the extra weight on her.

"I take it you like what you see?" Storm asked, standing up from where she was sitting and spinning around for Luck to view her ensemble from head to toe.

"I love what I see. Shit, we about to be working on baby number three."

"Hell no! Hell no!" Storm protested. She was done with having more kids. Sage completed their family and the sooner Luck realized that, the better off they would be.

"You say that now..." Luck started, walking up on Storm to whisper in her ear to ensure that Lauryn wouldn't hear what he was about to say. "But when I hit your spot, you'll be saying something entirely different."

Blushing, Storm couldn't protest... and even if she could, she wouldn't. Luck was right, when they were in the moment and he was hitting her spot the way she liked, she'd agree to whatever Lucky wanted her to do.

"That's what I thought..." Strutting away with his signature bop, Storm couldn't do much but admire her husband. Once Lucky had made it into the closet area to get dressed out of the view of Lauryn, Storm diverted her attention to Lauryn and Sage.

Grabbing Sage's clothes, Storm prepared herself for the fight she knew she was about to have with her youngest child. He would raise hell for the next hour being that she was waking him up out of his sleep, but she had no choice. Dinner reservations were made for 7:45 p.m. and it was already 6:30 p.m. She had let him sleep as long as she possibly could. Now, it was time to get him together.

Smiling inwardly at the fussing and crying Sage carried on with while she changed his diaper and got him dressed, she couldn't help but feel complete. This was life... this was her life. She was thankful for every high and low that she had experienced within the past year. They brought her to the place she was currently at. With her two beautiful children and her handsome husband. Yeah, they'd had a hell of a time, but she'd go through it all again just to have the same outcome she was experiencing in this moment.

6 MONTHS LATER

"I MOVE FORWARD, THE ONLY DIRECTION..."

-Jay Z

"*A*utumn! Hi, my beauty!" Storm said with her attention focused solely on Autumn in the backseat. After Autumn had responded, Storm focused her attention on Amber before asking her, "What the hell are you doing here, Amber?" Storm, Autumn and Amber were pulling away from LAX.

Storm had received a phone call six and a half hours ago, as Amber and Autumn were boarding a plane to Los Angeles, alerting her of their arrival time and the gate to be at.

Not having the time to really ask Amber all of the questions that she wanted answers to, Storm waited patiently for the arrival time to near before she hoped in her truck and found her way to LAX to wait for her sister and niece.

"We're moving." Amber said like it was no big deal, head buried in her phone.

"Moving? Moving where?" Storm was perplexed. Surely there was no way they were moving to Los Angeles and this was the first time that she was hearing of it. She spoke to Amber and Erin every single day... why had no one informed her of this move?

"Here, silly!" Amber said like Storm should have known that already. Why else would she be in Los Angeles right now?

"Well, why the hell am I just finding this out? When are you moving? What did Steven have to say about this? Where are you going to stay? What about work?" Storm blurted question after question without taking a breath. She was angry and excited all at the same time. Amber moving to Los Angeles meant she would have one of her partners in crime with her at all times.

"Well damn, which one do you want me to answer first?"

"Answer all of them!" Storm was mad that she was driving at the moment and not sitting in the passenger's seat. Amber deserved her undivided attention because clearly, a lot had transpired that Storm was not aware of.

Amber and Steven were just about divorced... actually, they were only waiting on the papers they had signed to be processed.

For the past six months, Steven had fought hard for his wife and his marriage but in the end, it turned out to not be enough. Amber stood by her decision and her word. She was tired of dealing with the same things she had been encountering since she was a teenager.

Giving Steven another chance was out of the question. Her giving him chance after chance was the reason why she was in the predicament that she was in now. There was no way she would give him another option to hurt her. That was completely out of the question.

"Steven doesn't quite know that we are moving... he thinks we're coming to visit you, Luck and the kids. You know, for vacation... I found an apartment that I'm going to view tomorrow before I put the security deposit and shit down on it. For now, I have no idea where I am going to work but I've been looking at spaces and have a few I want to check out over the next few days. Thanks to you, I was able to save a pretty penny by having my rent paid up for a couple of months so I'm looking for a shop now."

"Wow, you are really serious. You have all of this planned out?" Storm asked, not too sure how to feel. Amber never left her out of anything, but here she was making a move this big and Storm was completely out of the loop. "Why didn't you tell me?"

"I wanted to figure this out on my own first. I knew if I told you, you would take control of everything. You would have been just as excited as me and wouldn't have been able to stop yourself. I wanted to do this for Autumn and I. Hell, the only person who knows beside you is Erin and that's only because she drove us to the airport. She literally found out the way you found out. A phone call a little before we needed to be getting to the airport and I swore her to secrecy. I have to figure out how I'm going to break this news to Steven. I know he's going to have a fit." Amber stressed over what the conversation was going to be like with Steven. He would probably try to take her to court for custody or some shit. Amber wasn't ready to face the music that she knew Steven would bring just yet.

After taking time to process what Amber had said, Storm nodded her head. She understood where Amber was coming from and it was true. If Storm knew that Amber was even considering moving, Storm would have had everything figured out already. She couldn't be mad at Amber for wanting to do this on her own, hell, she had kept her relocation to New York a secret as well. How dare she take Amber's decision personal.

"I understand where you're coming from and I can't blame you. I would have been all over everything." Storm laughed.

"Yeah, I know. You don't let nothing slide through. I would have had a place, a job, a car, a man and more." Amber joked.

"Shit, you are right about that!" Storm confirmed.

When they were stopped at a red light, Storm reached over and grabbed Amber before pulling her into a tight hug. "I'm so glad you're here, sister! This is gonna be so much fun!"

"BABE! BABE! GUESS WHO'S HERE!" Storm shouted throughout the house as Amber and Autumn followed her throughout the foyer and into the immaculate living room.

Dropping their bags at the entrance of the living room, the three of them went to the couch and took a seat.

Minutes passed before Luck came down the stairs with Sage in his arms and Lauryn trailing behind him. Looking at the three of them making their way down the staircase, Amber smiled. She loved Storm and Luck together, they complimented each other so well.

Autumn and Lauryn both rushed each other with hugs before they were hand in hand running to Lauryn's room to play.

"What the hell are you doing here?" Luck asked, sounding like Storm.

"I decided to move here to be closer to you guys." Amber told him as she stood up and made her way to him. Taking Sage from his arms, Amber flooded his face with kisses.

With his mouth hung wide open and shock evident on his face, Luck didn't really know what to say. That became evident when the next question flew from his mouth. "Does Steven know?"

"What does Steven knowing have to do with me moving? I'm grown and two seconds short of being divorced." Annoyance dripped from Am's voice. She was over everyone asking about

Steven and whether he knew. The only thing they shared at this point was their last name and their child.

"No offense, sis. I'm just asking because Autumn is his daughter too. How would you feel if he had custody of her and he up and moved away six hours away without letting you know?"

Rolling her eyes, Amber inhaled deeply before releasing it and reclaiming her seat on the couch with Sage still in her arms.

"I hate it when you're right..."

"I love you too." Luck joked with Amber before finding a seat on the love seat across from Amber and Storm. "So, you serious about moving here?"

"Dead serious."

"Well, what do you need our help doing?"

Smiling, Storm and Amber couldn't help but think about how much they loved Luck. Regardless of what was going on, Luck was always front and center for them.

After running everything down to Lucky, the three of them got to work putting everything in place for the move. By the time they were done, Amber had a list of apartments and business properties that she would be viewing the next day. She also had a list of schools to view, new clientele and had scheduled for her belongings and car to be picked up and shipped to her.

"Alright, let me go and call this man and let him know my plan." Amber said, handing a now sleeping Sage off to Storm.

Grabbing her luggage, Luck helped her to the room she'd be staying in until everything was squared away with her apartment and then he found his way back to the living room.

"I know you're excited."

"I'm glad you know. My partner in crime is here to stayyyyy!" Storm sang.

"Yeah, alright. Just know I'll punish you in other ways if you two think y'all about to run like y'all used to run." Luck said making Storm crack up laughing.

"I'm a married woman, Sir. I take my vows seriously." Storm said, winking at him before standing up with Sage to take him to his room with Luck trailing behind her.

"Let me remind you about those vows really quick." Luck said, grabbing her ass as she made her way up the stairs.

"You better stop! If I drop my baby playing around with you it's on sight." Storm threatened.

"Well hurry your ass up and put him down then, meet me in our room. You know the routine... no clothes on, face down, ass up."

Blushing, Storm put a pep in her step anticipating the sex session they were about to embark on.

The last six months had been blissful for them. Storm was thankful for all of the time and effort that they had put into rebuilding their marriage. They were still in counseling—individually and jointly, working on their communication. They had a date night religiously once a week and a family night once a week as well. They were dedicated to making their marriage work. The six months they spent apart was long enough to last a lifetime.

Understandably, divorce was an answer for some, but it would never be an answer for them. They were made to be with each other and that's how they planned on keeping it.

ABOUT SKY EM

Sky EM is a five-time, self-published author of titles under the genres of Urban Fiction and Self-Help. She is also the co-author and publisher of 'Jus Chubb's Alkaline Non-Recipe Cookbook'.

Sky EM is a Brooklyn native, currently residing in Los Angeles, whose passion for writing started in her early childhood.

As a child, Sky EM could always be found with a piece of paper and a pen in hand, writing everything from journal entries to poetry. However, writing for her became a passion when her brother passed the summer before she entered High School.

What started as a class project, quickly evolved into a way of life. From talent shows to poetry slams, awards and performing on many stages in NYC, it was evident that when her pen hit paper, or her voice touched a mic it was something magical.

Sky EM plans to paint the world with her words, bringing to life the world as she sees it.

Stay connected with Sky by joining her on social media!

facebook.com/MiSSEIYESE
twitter.com/liVElOVESKY
instagram.com/iamskyem
amazon.com/author/ms.skyem

www.ingramcontent.com/pod-product-compliance
Lightning Source LLC
Chambersburg PA
CBHW050418260626
47156CB00003B/1064